James Hadley Chase and The Murder Room

››› This title is part of The Murder Room, our series dedicated to making available out-of-print or hard-to-find titles by classic crime writers.

Crime fiction has always held up a mirror to society. The Victorians were fascinated by sensational murder and the emerging science of detection; now we are obsessed with the forensic detail of violent death. And no other genre has so captivated and enthralled readers.

Vast troves of classic crime writing have for a long time been unavailable to all but the most dedicated frequenters of second-hand bookshops. The advent of digital publishing means that we are now able to bring you the backlists of a huge range of titles by classic and contemporary crime writers, some of which have been out of print for decades.

From the genteel amateur private eyes of the Golden Age and the femmes fatales of pulp fiction, to the morally ambiguous hard-boiled detectives of mid twentieth-century America and their descendants who walk our twenty-first century streets, The Murder Room has it all. **›››**

The Murder Room
Where Criminal Minds Meet

themurderroom.com

James Hadley Chase (1906–1985)

Born René Brabazon Raymond in London, the son of a British colonel in the Indian Army, James Hadley Chase was educated at King's School in Rochester, Kent, and left home at the age of 18. He initially worked in book sales until, inspired by the rise of gangster culture during the Depression and by reading James M. Cain's *The Postman Always Rings Twice*, he wrote his first novel, *No Orchids for Miss Blandish*. Despite the American setting of many of his novels, Chase (like Peter Cheyney, another hugely successful British noir writer) never lived there, writing with the aid of maps and a slang dictionary. He had phenomenal success with the novel, which continued unabated throughout his entire career, spanning 45 years and nearly 90 novels. His work was published in dozens of languages and over thirty titles were adapted for film. He served in the RAF during World War II, where he also edited the RAF Journal. In 1956 he moved to France with his wife and son; they later moved to Switzerland, where Chase lived until his death in 1985.

By James Hadley Chase
(published in The Murder Room)

By James Hadley Chase
(published in The Hadley Region...)

No Orchids for Miss Blandish
Eve
More Deadly Than the Male
Mission to Venice
Mission to Siena
Not Safe to Be Free
Shock Treatment
Come Easy – Go Easy
What's Better Than Money?
Just Another Sucker
I Would Rather Stay Poor
A Coffin from Hong Kong
Tell it to the Birds
One Bright Summer Morning
The Soft Centre
You Have Yourself a Deal
Have This One on Me
Well Now, My Pretty
Believed Violent
An Ear to the Ground
The Whiff of Money
The Vulture is a Patient Bird
Like a Hole in the Head

An Ace Up My Sleeve
Want to Stay Alive?
Just the Way It Comes
You're Dead Without Money
Have a Change of Scene
Knock, Knock! Who's There?
Goldfish Have No Hiding Place
So What Happens to Me?
The Joker in the Pack
Believe This, You'll Believe Anything
Do Me a Favour, Drop Dead
I Hold the Four Aces
My Laugh Comes Last
Consider Yourself Dead
You Must Be Kidding
We'll Share a Double Funeral
Try This One for Size
You Can Say That Again
Hand Me a Fig Leaf
Have a Nice Night
We'll Share a Double Funeral
Not My Thing
Hit Them Where It Hurts

The Soft Centre

James Hadley Chase

An Orion book

Copyright © Hervey Raymond 1975

The right of James Hadley Chase to be identified as the author of this
work has been asserted in accordance with the Copyright, Designs and
Patents Act 1988.

This edition published by
The Orion Publishing Group Ltd
Orion House
5 Upper St Martin's Lane
London WC2H 9EA

An Hachette UK company
A CIP catalogue record for this book is available from the British Library

ISBN 978 1 4719 0354 0

www.orionbooks.co.uk

Chapter One

VALERIE BURNETT lay in the bath, her head against the padded head-rest, her eyes closed.

Through the half open window came the sound of distant voices from the terrace below. It was a cheerful sound, and Valerie was glad to listen to it. She was glad too that they had come to this hotel in Spanish Bay: it was everything that had been said about it. It really was, she thought, the nicest hotel she had ever been to, and she had been to so many, she couldn't try to enumerate them.

She opened her eyes and looked down at her long beautifully formed body. Her full breasts and a small strip of flesh across her hips were startlingly white against the rest of her golden tan.

They had been in Spanish Bay for only a week, but the sun had been excitingly hot and she had tanned quickly and without burning.

She lifted a wet hand and picked up the gold and platinum watch that Chris had given to her for a wedding present. She saw it was twenty minutes to twelve. She would have time to dress leisurely and then go down to the terrace for an ice cold martini. She still hadn't quite adjusted herself to drinking martinis when Chris now only drank tomato juice. In some odd way, it made her feel guilty that he could no longer drink alcohol, but the doctor had warned her that she must continue to act and live normally as it would be bad for Chris to know that, because of him, she was altering her previous way of life.

1

As she put the watch back on the table by the bath, the telephone bell rang. She dried her hand on a towel and lifted the receiver.

"There's a call from New York," the operator told her. "Will you take it, Mrs. Burnett?"

No one but her father knew they were at the Spanish Bay hotel, so it must be her father calling, Val thought.

"Yes," she said, and her brows moved into a small crease of worry and irritation. She had asked her father to leave them alone. Well, all right, he had done so for a week. It was her fault he should be calling. She hadn't written to him, and she should have done, knowing how anxious he always was about her.

Her father's voice came over the line. He had a deep impressive voice. She often thought when listening to him talk that if he hadn't become a tycoon, he would have made a magnificent Shakespearean actor.

"Val? You there?"

"Why, hello, Daddy. It's nice . . ."

"Val! I've been waiting to hear from you!"

"I'm sorry. You know how it is. The sun has been wonderful. I know I should . . ."

"Never mind that. How is Chris?"

"Oh . . . well, he's fine. We were only talking about you last night and he . . ."

"I want to know how he is. Look, Val. I have a meeting in five minutes. Don't waste time. How is he?"

She moved her long legs in the water impatiently.

"Darling, I've just told you. He's fine."

"I think it was a mistake for you to be down there alone with him. He's still a sick man, Val. Tell me: has he still got that goddamn tick around his mouth?"

Val closed her eyes. The water seemed to be getting very cold or perhaps it was her body was turning cold.

"It is much better," she said. "Really . . ."

"But he's still got it?"

"Well, yes, but it's . . ."

"Does he sit around still like a zombie?"

Aware that tears were filling her eyes, Val said, "He—he still likes to sit and do nothing, but I know it will be all right. I know he is much better."

"What does Dr. Gustave say about him?"

Val reached forward and twisted the knob to release the water in the bath.

"He said Chris is improving, but it would take time."

"Time! Well, for God's sake, he has been acting like a zombie now for eighteen months!"

"I wish you wouldn't say things like that, Daddy. I know how long it has been, but it really isn't so long considering what . . ."

"It's too long. Look, Valerie, you're twenty-five with all the instincts of a normal, healthy woman. You can't go on living like this. It isn't fair to you. I worry about you. You can't be tied to a man who . . ."

"Daddy!" Her voice suddenly became sharp. "I love Chris! I'm his wife! I won't listen to this kind of talk! I mean that! It's not your business! It's mine!"

There was a pause, then her father said in a more gentle tone, "I love you too, Val. I can't help worrying. All right, I understand. I won't make it harder for you, but I must know what is going on. I rely on you to tell me, and remember if there is anything I can do. I want to do it . . . anything."

"Thanks, Daddy, yes, of course, but I can really and truly handle this thing." She pulled the towel over her as she lay in the empty bath. "I'm getting cold, darling. I'm in my bath."

"What's Chris doing?"

"He's on the terrace reading *Oliver Twist*," Val said. "He's discovered Charles Dickens. He's bought the whole set and he's reading right the way through."

"Well . . ." There was a pause, then Val heard a murmur of voices over the line, then her father said, "I have to go, Val. You are sure you can handle this?"

"Yes."

"Don't forget . . . if you want me, call me. I'll be back at the office around five o'clock. You can't reach me before as I'll be moving around, but . . ."

" Why should I want you, darling?"

" Just remember. My love, Val . . . 'bye."

She hung up and got out of the bath, aware she was very cold. She briskly towelled herself, and then slipping into a blue and white polka dot wrap, she walked quickly into the big bedroom and out onto the balcony that overlooked the beautiful bay with its coves, its miles of sands and its sun umbrellas. She looked down at the terrace where Chris had been sitting.

The lounging chair was empty. The blue covered copy of *Oliver Twist* lay open on the green paving of the terrace.

With sudden fear gripping her heart, she looked frantically up and down the length of the terrace at the groups of people drinking and talking and the white-coated waiters who moved to the various tables, carrying drinks, to the big doorman standing in the sun in his white tropical uniform, and beyond him to the gently moving sea and the almost deserted sands, but she could see no sign of Chris.

Spanish Bay hotel was one of the most expensive and luxurious hotels in Florida. It catered only for fifty guests, but offered them a service that more than justified the cost so high that only the extremely wealthy could afford to stay there.

Charles Travers, Val's father, had chosen the hotel. As the doctors had said that Chris needed quiet, relaxation and pampering, Travers said this was the obvious hotel for them to stay at. He had arranged everything. The bill was to be sent to him, and he even had given them a Mercedes convertible for a runabout during their stay.

Val would have preferred to have gone to a less luxurious hotel as she knew her father was by now irritated that Chris could no longer support his wife in the way a multi-millionaire's daughter should be supported. However, the hotel was so perfect that she quickly forgot her scruples, and was glad her father had insisted on them going there.

Their first week's stay had been without incident. She had

4

come to accept the fact that Chris had lost all his initiative, that he appeared completely happy just to sit in the sun, to read and to talk to her in a vague way about anything that wasn't personal to themselves. That they had separate bedrooms, and he never showed any desire to touch her, gave her a hollow feeling of frustration, but this was something she could and did cope with. When they first arrived, she kept a close watch on him. This wasn't difficult as the hotel was so situated that you could see for miles across the sands, and there was no way of reaching the nearest town unless by car. She kept the igni-tion key of the car always in her bag, and out of Chris's reach

But as the days passed, and Chris seemed content just to read and sunbathe, she realised now, she had become complacent and careless. She should never have let him sit on the terrace alone, she told herself as she slipped into a pair of beach slacks. As she pulled on a cotton sweater, she suddenly thought of the car key, and she ran across the room to where her bag was lying. With shaking hands, she opened the bag and searched for the key but couldn't find it. She dumped the contents of the bag onto the dressing-table and looked again. She realised with a feeling of panic that Chris must have come to her room when she was in the bath and taken the key.

She went out onto the balcony and looked towards the car park at the far end of the terrace. The white Mercedes was missing.

She returned to the bedroom and hastily ran a comb through her hair.

You're panicking for nothing, she told herself. He'll be back. Why shouldn't he go for a drive if he feels like it? I said I would be down at half past twelve. It's not twelve yet. He pro-bably got bored with his book and went for a little drive. But she knew she was thinking nonsense. Chris had refused to touch any car since the accident and she had always done the driv-ing. Why had he waited until she was in the bath before sneak-ing in and taking the key unless something . . . something . . .

Unable to contain her panic, she snatched up her bag and hurried down the long corridor to the elevator.

She pressed the call button and immediately the green light appeared. A moment later the cage came to rest before her.

The boy, immaculate in white, said, " Good morning, madam : lounge floor?"

" Yes, please," Val said and leaned against the mirror that ran the length of the wall of the cage.

They sank between floors, then the doors swung open and Val walked quickly across the vast, luxurious lounge to the revolving doors.

As she came out onto the terrace, the doorman saluted her.

She looked up and down, but there was still no sign of Chris. She hesitated for a moment, then trying to control the shake in her voice, she said to the doorman, " I thought Mr. Burnett was on the terrace. Did he go somewhere?"

She prayed silently that the doorman would say Chris was in the Men's room or in the bar or somewhere in the hotel, but the doorman said Mr. Burnett had taken the car and had driven towards Miami.

" About ten minutes ago, madam."

" Thank you," Val said and walked slowly along the terrace to where Chris had left his book. She sat down in the lounging chair and picked up the book. She opened her handbag and took out a pair of sunglasses which she put on.

A waiter same up silently and placed a dry martini on the table beside her. Part of the service of this hotel was to anticipate their client's wishes. This could be a little irritating, but this time, Val needed a drink.

" Will Mr. Burnett require tomato juice, madam?" the waiter asked.

" I expect so," Val said, not looking at him. " He's out right now."

The waiter went away and Val picked up her drink and sipped it. She sat for some moments staring across the sands and at the sea, aware of her pounding heart and the sick feeling of fear like a hard ball inside her. She looked at her watch. It was now a quarter past twelve. She mustn't do a thing, she told herself, until half-past twelve : that was the time she had told Chris she would be joining him. If she did start something and he arrived back to greet her and he found out she had panicked, she would do untold damage. The doctor had warned her she must show confidence in Chris. Well, all right, she would show confidence.

She sat there, waiting. At the sound of every approaching car, she stiffened and looked anxiously towards the long drive that led down to the main gates of the hotel. People were returning now for lunch and the doorman was busy saluting and opening car doors. None of the cars that swept up the drive was a white Mercedes convertible.

At half-past twelve, she had finished her martini. She was now gripping the copy of *Oliver Twist* so tightly, her fingers were aching.

I'll wait ten more minutes, she told herself, then I'll have to do something . . . but what?

The waiter came over to her: another dry martini looking lonely, but very cold and tempting on his tray.

"Perhaps another, madam?" he asked cautiously. She had never had more than one dry martini before lunch, but the waiter seemed to sense she needed a second. This was proof again of the superb service the hotel offered.

"Why, yes . . . thank you. I think I will," Val said.

The martini was placed by her side, the empty glass removed. The waiter silently walked away.

Val looked at her watch. She reached for the glass and sipped the drink and put the glass back on the table.

He isn't coming, she thought. Oh, God! What *am* I going to do? Daddy said he wouldn't be around until five o'clock. If only I knew where . . . no! I mustn't tell *him*! He's the very, very last person I will tell. But who can help me? Dr. Gustave? Yes, perhaps I'd better call him. But what can he do? I can't expect him to go rushing all over the place looking for Chris. The police? They could find him, but once they know who Chris is, the newspapers will get onto his disappearance and then . . . oh, no! I'm not going to start that awful publicity all over again.

7

Again she looked at her watch. It showed twelve forty-five. She heard an approaching car and she leaned forward to watch a Rolls Royce glide up to the entrance of the hotel. A fat woman, carrying a fat Pekingese, descended and walked slowly and heavily up the steps to the terrace.

He could be here any moment, Val thought. I just mustn't panic. I must have faith. I'll wait until one o'clock, then I really, really *must* do something.

A few minutes to one o'clock, she saw Jean Dulac, the manager of the hotel, coming along the terrace : a tall, handsome man with impeccable manners and the polished charm that is unique to the French. He paused at each table to exchange a word with his guests.

Val watched him come. It was a little after one o'clock before he finally reached her table.

" Madame Burnett . . . alone?" He smiled down at her. " But this is quite wrong." Then he paused, looking sharply at her white, strained face. " Perhaps there is something I can do? Can I help you?"

" I hope you can," Val said shakily. " Please sit down. I . . ."

" No, I won't do that. People here have nothing else to do but to observe and gossip. Please come, in a few moments, to my office." He smiled at her. " Your worries are naturally my worries. Come and let me see what I can do." He gave her a little bow and moved on.

She waited a long and painful interval. Then as people began to leave their tables and move towards the restaurant, she got up and walked with controlled slowness to Dulac's office.

The office was behind the reception desk. A clerk, busy with an adding machine, paused to give her a bow as she came up to the counter.

" Please go right on in, Mrs. Burnett," he said " Monsieur Dulac is waiting for you."

She went into the big room with windows overlooking the bay. It was a gracious room with flowers, comfortable furniture and a small desk at which Dulac was sitting. He rose at once as she came in and led her to a chair.

8

"Sit down," he said. "Now we can cope with the problem between us, Madame. It's Mr. Burnett?"

Val sat down. She had a sudden urge to cry and she had to struggle hard not to break down.

Dulac walked to the window and paused there for a moment, then returned to his desk. He gave her enough time to control herself before going on. "I have had quite a lot of unhappiness in my own life, but looking back, I have always found there is a solution to most problems. Mr. Burnett has driven away and you are very worried about what has happened to him. That is the problem, is it not?"

"Then you know about my husband?"

"I know about all the people who stay with me. How else could I serve them?"

"He's—he's gone and I'm very frightened."

"He has been away over an hour." Dulac shook his head. "That is too long. We must consult the police."

Val flinched, but Dulac lifted his hand.

"I assure you you don't have to worry about unwanted publicity. If you will allow me, I will arrange everything. Captain Terrell, the Chief of Police, is a good friend of mine. He is understanding and will take immediate action in the most tactful way possible. You can be quite sure he will not only find Mr. Burnett quickly, but no one besides ourselves will be any the wiser. I can promise you that."

Val drew in a long, deep breath.

"Thank you. Yes, of course . . . I'll leave it to you. I'm very, very grateful."

"Everything that can be done will be done," Dulac said, getting to his feet. "Now may I suggest you go to your suite? I'll have a tray sent up to you." He smiled as Val began to protest. "Something very light, but you must eat, you know." He led her to the door. "In half-an-hour, Captain Terrell will be with you."

Captain Frank Terrell was a large man with sandy hair flecked with white. His heavy featured face ended in a jutting, square

9

jaw and his eyes were steel grey. He was well liked by the men who served under him and feared by the criminals who infested the rich stamping ground of Greater Miami.

He sat in an armchair that was dwarfed by his bulk and looked thoughtfully at Val as she sat opposite him, her hands gripped tightly between her knees.

"Dulac has told me something about this problem, Mrs. Burnett," he said. There was a gentle note in his usually stern voice. "I have already sent out a description of your husband and his car. I have no doubt that within an hour or so one of my men will find him. I want to assure you that you have nothing to worry about."

Val said, "Thank you . . . the newspapers . . ."

"You don't have to worry about them. I know how to deal with reporters," Terrell said. "Dulac tells me your husband isn't very well. He didn't go into details. Would you care to tell me a little more about him?"

"Why, yes . . . if—if you think it is necessary," Val said.

"What exactly is the matter with him?"

"Two years ago he had a motor accident. He suffered severe head injuries. He was unconscious for over five months. Before the accident he was a brilliant man and worked with my father. When he came out of the coma, he—he . . . well, to use my father's words, he acted like a zombie." Val paused and looked out of the window, struggling to control her tears. "He spent months in a sanatorium. Nothing anyone did seemed to help him. There was nothing physically wrong with him, but he just lost interest in everything . . . including me. He remained in the sanatorium for about eighteen months. He neither got better nor worse. I decided I couldn't leave him there, and against my father's wishes, I insisted that we should try to give him a more normal life in the hope, away from the sanatorium, he would make a recovery. The doctors agreed. So I brought him here. We have been here a week, and he did begin to show a little improvement."

"In what way?" Terrell asked.

"He began to take an interest in certain limited things. Before he came here, he would just sit and stare into space for hours. Here, he found a copy of *Oliver Twist* and he began to read it. He asked me to get him the complete works of Dickens which I did. He planned to read right through Dickens. He also began to show interest in the people here : discussing them with me."

" Did he show any awakening interest in you?"

Val lifted her hands helplessly.

" No."

" I understand he has consulted Dr. Gustave," Terrell went on after a pause. " Why did he do that?"

" He has been in the hands of doctors for two years. He hasn't any confidence in himself. He seems to feel lost without a doctor close at hand."

" I know Dr. Gustave well," Terrell said. " He is a good man. What did he think of your husband?"

" Oh, he said he showed signs of improvement, but it would take a long time."

" He didn't warn you that your husband could suddenly run off like this?"

" No."

" Wasn't your husband nervous about driving a car when he came out of the sanatorium?"

" That is one of the things that is worrying me. He hasn't touched a car since the accident . . . until this morning. I have always done the driving."

Terrell thought for a moment, then got to his feet.

" As soon as we have found him, I'll let you know. Perhaps it would be better for you to come to headquarters and bring him back here yourself. I guess Dr. Gustave should be alerted. I'll handle that. You must try to relax. It won't take long to find him. I have men patrolling all the main highways leading out to Miami."

When he had gone, Val sat down near the window where she could watch the drive below, and began her long wait.

Chapter Two

SERGEANT JOE BEIGLER ran stubby fingers through his close cut hair, a frown of concentration on his freckled face. He sat at a battered desk in a large room that contained other desks at which uniformed policemen worked, talked into telephones or scribbled in notebooks.

Beigler was reading through a report to do with a minor jewel robbery. He was the senior Sergeant and Terrell's right hand man. Unmarried, aged thirty-eight, an addict to coffee drinking and cigarette smoking, he was regarded by his Chief as the best Sergeant he had had in years.

The telephone bell tinkled and he dropped a large, hairy hand on the receiver, picked it up and growled, "Yeah? . . . Beigler."

"The Chief's just come in," the Desk Sergeant said. "In his office now."

Beigler grunted, tossed the file he had been studying into his Pending tray and walking with heavy strides, he made his way to Terrell's office.

He found Terrell about to pour coffee from a can one of his men had just brought to him. Seeing Beigler in the doorway, Terrell took another cup from his desk drawer and filled that too.

"Come on in, Joe. Anything on the Burnett business?"

Beigler came in, closed the door and sat on the straight back chair before Terrell's desk. As he reached for the cup of coffee, he said, "Nothing yet. Every patrol has been alerted. What's the excitement about?"

Terrell began to fill a blackened and well-used pipe.

"Important people. The guy's the son-in-law of Charles Travers, and in case you don't know who he is, he's the one who built the New York Palace hotel, a ferry bridge, a dam in Havana and a number of little items of the same weight and standing."

Beigler drank some of the coffee, then lit a cigarette.

"So?"

"So we have to find the guy. There's a complication." Terrell paused while he puffed at his pipe. "He's a mental case. On my way back from talking to his wife, I dropped in on Dr. Gustave who knows about the case. This guy sustained bad injuries to his head in a car smash. Dr. Gustave says there are brain adhesions. They could clear up, given time, but in the meantime, he's not responsible for his actions. He hasn't driven a car for two years, and now he's in a Mercedes somewhere on his own. He could cause a lot of damage to himself and to others in a car as fast as a Mercedes."

"What do you want me to do?" Beigler asked, finishing his coffee. "Put another call out to the boys?"

"I guess so. Tell them this is urgent. I want this guy found and found fast! It's more than two hours since we put the first call out. Can't be all that hard to find a white convertible Mercedes."

"He could have taken to the dirt roads," Beigler said, getting to his feet.

"I don't give a damn what he's done. I want him found pronto!"

Beigler nodded and went down to the Operations room. He sat at a desk, picked up a microphone and began calling the patrol cars. Even as he began to talk, an officer came up and touched him on the shoulder.

"Harry's calling, Sarg. He's found the Mercedes."

Beigler handed over the mike.

"Tell the boys," he said and went over to another desk. He picked up the telephone receiver lying on the desk.

"Harry?"

"Yes, Sarg. I found the car: White Mercedes. Licence No. 33567. Registered New York on the Old Dixie highway. Bust off side tyre: on side fender smashed. Skid marks across the road. The car finished up against a tree. Must have been travelling fast."

Beigler rubbed the end of his nose.

"The driver?"

"No one in the car, Sarg."

"Hold it," Beigler snapped and swivelled around in his chair. "Hi, Jack, how many cars we got near the Old Dixie highway?"

"Three." The plotter who kept tabs on all the patrol cars informed him. "Two within twenty miles: the third within ten miles."

"Tell them to converge on Harry and fast. He'll want help." Beigler went on to Harry. "Three cars are on their way. I want a thorough search of the district. The driver can't be far away. You stay where you are. Bud will give you a description of the guy." He beckoned to another officer, handed over the telephone receiver and went quickly back to Terrell's office.

At twenty minutes to three in the afternoon, Val was still sitting by the window and still waiting. She kept telling herself that there was nothing she could do, and she just had to be patient till the police found Chris. But as the time moved on, she became more and more anxious. This lone vigil was beginning to tear her nerves to shreds. She was already asking herself if Chris had met with another accident . . . this time, was he dead?

Suddenly the telephone bell buzzed. For a moment she just stared at the instrument, then getting to her feet, she ran over and lifted the receiver.

"Mrs. Burnett . . . this is Captain Terrell."

"Have—have you found him?"

"Not yet, but we have found the car," Terrell told her. "It was found on the Old Dixie highway . . . not often used these days. Had a burst tyre and hit a tree. Looks as if your husband left the car and started to walk. I have four cars out there and our men are searching the district. It's difficult country : lots of shrub land, orchards, disused barns. He might have gone into some derelict building to rest. I thought I'd let you know what's happening. Don't worry. We'll find him soon."

" But he might be injured and . . ."

" I don't think so. It wasn't a bad enough smash for that. Just a bent fender. He's probably a bit dazed and is resting somewhere."

" Perhaps I had better come. I could get a taxi and . . ."

" Best for you to remain where you are, Mrs. Burnett," Terrell said firmly. " Then we'll know where you are. As soon as we've found him. I'll call again."

" All right . . . thank you for calling me."

" You're welcome," Terrell said, a little embarrassed to hear how unsteady her voice sounded. " Shouldn't be long now," and he hung up.

Val went over to the window and looked out across the sea. There were a number of people sunning themselves and swimming. It was a gay scene, but there was no gaiety in Val's heart.

When there was no call from police headquarters at five o'clock she began to get desperate.

She waited until twenty minutes past five, then unable to bear the suspense any longer, she put a call through to her father's New York office.

From babyhood, Val's relations with her father had been on good, sound terms. She had come to worship this successful, handsome man. She had always been convinced that he could solve any of her problems once she appealed for help. She had been careful in the past to appeal to him on only the very important things, and they had been few, but each time she had appealed to him, he had dropped everything and had put the whole of his massive energy into solving the problem. She was sure that the reason why he was so impatient with Chris was because Chris presented a problem that defeated him : the first problem to do with Val he hadn't been able to solve.

15

After a ten minute wait, she got his office and was told by his secretary that he was in conference.

"This is Mrs. Burnett. Will you please tell my father I must speak to him immediately?"

"Yes, of course, Mrs. Burnett. Will you hold on? It may be a few minutes. I'll have to send in a note."

What were a few minutes, Val thought, after all these awful, never ending hours?

"I'll hold on."

Less than five minutes crawled by before her father's voice came on the line.

"Val."

"Daddy, he's gone! I'm frantic! After I had spoken to you, I looked out of the window and he had gone!"

"Did he take the car?"

She drew in a deep breath. Her father's voice was calm. She had expected him to fly in a rage : to tell her he had warned her, but this practical, quiet question had an immediate steadying effect on her.

"Yes. He's been missing now for over five hours."

"Have you consulted Dulac?"

"Yes. He got the Chief of Police here. The police have found the Mercedes, but not Chris."

"Are they still looking?"

"I suppose so . . . I don't know."

"Tell the operator to hold this call and then call the police. I want to know what the position is right now!"

"I'll do that. Oh, darling, do you think . . . ?"

"Val! Do what I say! Don't let's waste time!"

She got the operator to hold the New York call and then put her through to Terrell.

"Have you any news?" she asked when Terrell came on the line. "My father . . ."

"No news yet, Mrs. Burnett." Val was quick to hear a worried note in Terrell's voice. "My men are still looking, but out there, it's difficult country. I can't spare more than eight men. Frankly, if we are to find your husband before dark, we'll have to get help, and this will mean publicity. I was about to call you when you came through. What do you want me to do?"

Val tried to think, then she said unsteadily, " I'll call you back." She asked the operator to give her New York again. " They haven't found him," she told her father. " I told the Chief of Police I didn't want any publicity. He says if we are to find Chris before dark, he'll have to get help : then the news-papers will hear about it."

" Tell him to get help," Travers said. " Tell him I expect to find Chris with you when I arrive. I'm flying down right away. I'll be with you as soon as I possibly can. Don't worry, Val. I'm on my way."

" But, darling, aren't you terribly tied up? Has Newton . . .?"

" We're wasting time ! I'm coming ! Just tell this policeman to get all the help he needs. Stay in your suite. Tell Dulac to handle the press. I'll fix everything when I arrive. God bless," and the line went dead.

Val called Terrell.

" My father is coming down. Will you get all the help you need? We must find my husband tonight."

" Yes, of course," Terrell said. " I'm sorry about this, Mrs. Burnett, but we're just not getting the breaks. It'll be on the radio in half-an-hour. I'll get the farmers to search all their out-buildings. We'll check the motels, hospitals and hotels. The press will have to come into it."

" Yes," Val said and hung up.

She put her hands to her face. After a while she began to cry.

The gold and green enamel clock on the overmantel in Val's sitting-room struck eleven.

Val lay on the settee by the open window, looking out at the starlit sky. It was a dark night : there was no moon.

Her father sat near her in a lounging chair, a whisky and soda on the occasional table by his side, a cigar smouldering be-tween his fingers.

Neither of them had said anything to each other for the past half-hour. When her father had arrived, he had been unexpectedly kind and sympathetic. They had re-established the bond between them that had suffered since Chris had been in the sanatorium. Val now felt more relaxed. The presence of her father gave her confidence and acted as a solace.

Below in the hotel grounds, newspaper men and photographers had gathered. Val could hear the hum of their voices and now and then, there was a sudden sound of laughter that made her flinch.

Then out of the silence, the telephone bell buzzed. Travers picked up the receiver.

"Captain Terrell is here, sir," the clerk told him.

"Send him right up," Travers said and replaced the receiver. Val jumped to her feet and looked anxiously at him.

"Terrell coming up," her father said.

"Have they found him?"

"We'll know in a moment," her father said as he got to his feet.

At the age of sixty, Charles Travers was an impressive looking man. He was three inches over six foot, square shouldered and powerfully built. He had bright, searching blue eyes, thinning white hair and a lean hawk-like face. As he crossed the room, he gave Val renewed confidence by the power and assurance of his movements. He opened the door as Terrell came along the corridor.

The two men regarded each other, then shook hands.

"No news yet," Terrell said as he entered the room. " I thought I'd look in and tell you what we have been doing." He nodded to Val who stood by the settee, white-faced, her hands into fists.

"He's been missing over twelve hours," Travers said, a snap in his voice. " I certainly would be interested to know what you have been doing."

"I understand how you feel, Mr. Travers," Terrell said. "We can't do more than we are doing already. The country is very difficult. There are swamps, mangrove thickets, acres of high grass and hundreds of farm out-buildings. We have now combed the district five miles around from where the car was found. It seems we must consider two possibilities : either Mr. Burnett is deliberately hiding or he has managed to get a lift from a passing car that has taken him right out of the district. If he is deliberately hiding, then our task is almost impossible. There is no better ground to play hide-and-seek in. If he has left the district, then we must put out a four State alarm and appeal to all motorists who have been in this district to help us."

Travers stared searchingly at Terrell.

" What you are saying is bluntly this : you haven't the organisation to find a missing man in your territory."

"No State has an organisation to find a missing man quickly if he doesn't want to be found," Terrell said quietly. " But we will find him. It could take time."

"You don't expect to find him tonight?"

" I don't know. We could, but it now seems unlikely."

" That's all I want to know," Travers said. " All right, you carry on. We'll wait. Thank you for coming."

Feeling dismissed and irritated by Travers' manner, Terrell moved to the door, then he paused to look at Val.

" We'll find him, Mrs. Burnett. I would like to think you still have confidence in me."

"Oh, yes, I have," Val said shakily.

When Terrell had gone, her father put his arm around her and pulled her close to him.

" You're going to bed now," he said. " I'll be around. This is going to work out. You see . . . in a couple of weeks, probably less, you'll wonder why you got so worked up."

Val moved away from him.

"Daddy, you don't really understand. I can't thank you enough for coming. I can't thank you enough for your kindness and your help, but you still don't seem to realise that Chris is my life. I love him. I mean that . . . whatever he has become, however he behaves, he is now part of me. Without him, life would be meaningless to me. I'm telling you this because you don't seem able to accept the fact that he is so very, very important to me. He really and truly is all I now live for."

Travers looked thoughtfully at her, then with a little shrug of resignation, he said, " Come along, Val. You go to bed. You won't sleep, but you'll probably rest. They'll find him. While they are finding him, we'll sweat it out together."

Val put her hand affectionately on his arm.

" I just wanted to be sure you know how it is between Chris and myself. I'll go to bed. Thank you, darling. I don't know what I'd do without you."

She walked quickly across the room and into her bedroom. Travers moved to the window. He stood for a long moment staring out into the darkness, a frown on his face, then abruptly, he tossed his half-smoked cigar down onto the terrace where the newspaper men waited.

The smell of grilling ham made Terrell hasten with his shaving. He had stayed with the search for Burnett until three o'clock in the morning, then weary and discouraged, he had handed over to Beigler and had gone home.

As he finished shaving, he thought bleakly that Burnett couldn't have been found otherwise Joe would have telephoned. He thought of that nice Mrs. Burnett, and he felt sorry he had so far failed her. But what more could he have done? he asked himself.

When he entered the morning-room, he found his wife, Caroline, a large matronly looking woman, reading the newspaper headlines.

" Is it right this poor man is a mental case?" she asked, handing Terrell the paper.

" I guess," he said and sat down. " Trust the papers to get hold of the details. Now they will be scaring everyone out of their wits."

" But he isn't dangerous?"

Terrell shrugged.

" He's a mental case."

He sat and read, and finally tossed the paper aside in disgust.

" Where the hell can he have got to?" he said more to himself than to his wife. " What's he been doing all this time?"

As if to answer these questions, the telephone bell rang. Terrell put down his cup of coffee and hurried across the room. He lifted the receiver.

" Chief? This is Joe." Beigler's voice sounded tense. " We have trouble out at Ojus. A murder reported."

Terrell scratched his forehead. A murder! He hadn't had a murder in his territory for the past eight months.

" Any details, Joe?"

" The owner of the Park Motel phoned through. He reports a dead woman in one of his cabins. She's been badly cut up."

" Okay. Come out for me. Any news of Burnett?"

" The boys are still searching," Beigler was obviously bored with Burnett. A murder was much more important to him. " I have the team together. We'll be out for you in ten minutes."

Terrell hung up and returned to the table to finish his coffee. He told Caroline about the murder, but this didn't interest her. She wanted to know about Burnett.

" He's still missing," Terrell said irritably. " It's my guess he's miles away from where he smashed up the car. He must be. He probably had a blackout and has just gone off into the blue."

As two police cars pulled up outside Terrell's bungalow eight minutes later, and as Terrell was putting on his jacket, the telephone bell rang.

" Chief, this is Williams. We've found Burnett. He was wandering along the North Miami Beach highway. We have him here in our car. What shall we do with him?"

Aware that Beigler was standing in the doorway, scarcely restraining his impatience, Terrell said, " How is he?"

" Well, he acts as if he's been knocked on the head. He doesn't know where he's been nor what he's been doing."

" Stay right where you are," Terrell said. " I'll call you back." He broke the connection and then dialled the number of the Spanish Bay hotel. As he waited, he said to Beigler, " They've found Burnett. I have to fix him first. You go on to the Park Motel. I'll come on after you."

Beigler nodded and hurried down the flagged path to the waiting car.

When Terrell got the hotel, he asked to speak to Travers.

"Mr. Travers? Police Chief here. We've found Mr. Burnett. He seems in a dazed state. He is right at this moment in a police car out on the North Miami Beach highway : that's about thirty-five miles from you. I don't think it would be wise to bring him back to the hotel. He'd have to face the newspaper men who are waiting there. I suggest my men drive him straight to Dr. Gustave's sanatorium. Mrs. Burnett and you could meet him there. What do you think?"

"Yes," Travers said. "Thank you. We'll go over there right away."

"He'll be there within an hour," Terrell said. He broke the connection and got back to Williams. He gave him instructions, then briefly telling his wife what was happening, he hurried out to his car and drove fast towards the Park Motel at Ojus.

Ojus on U.S. highway 4 was originally an Indian trading post. Its name, in the Indian language, means "plentiful", and the town of some six hundred people was named so because of the luxuriant vegetation surrounding the place.

Just outside the town, on the main highway, was the Park Motel : second rate, but conveniently situated on the direct route to Miami. It consisted of forty small, shabby wooden cabins, a bathing pool, a Self-Service store, a children's sandpit and playing ground and a square of flattened ground where visitors could dance to the blaring swing coming from loud speakers strung up in the trees.

Terrell arrived at the motel five minutes after the police team had pulled in to the vast parking lot.

Fred Hess, in charge of the Homicide team, said Beigler was in the Reception office, talking to the owner.

Terrell told him to wait until he was ready and then walked across the rough grass that led to the cabin over which was a large neon sign that read :

PARK MOTEL
VACANCIES

Some ten to twelve men and women in holiday garb were standing near the office, gaping. They stared at Terrell as he entered the office, and there was an immediate buzz of conversation.

The hot, small office was divided by a counter on which lay the register, a telephone, several ball-point pens and an ashtray overflowing with cigarette butts.

Beyond the counter was a desk, three chairs and on the wall a large scale map of the district.

Beigler sat in one of the chairs, a cigarette hanging from his lips. Behind the desk sat the owner of the motel: a tall, thin man, around fifty-five, with a mop of iron grey hair and a sallow complexion. His face was thin with an over-long nose. His shabby grey Alpaca suit looked as if it was meant for a man of much heavier build. His white shirt was grubby and his string tie greasy.

"This is Henekey," Beigler said, getting to his feet. "Okay, Henekey, go ahead. Let's have it all over again."

Terrell nodded to Henekey who gave him a quick, uneasy stare. Terrell took a chair near Beigler.

"Well, like I told the Sergeant," Henekey said, "this girl had a call in for 7.30 a.m. I called her. There was no answer, so I went over and found her." He grimaced. "So I called headquarters."

"Who is she?" Terrell asked.

"She booked in as Sue Parnell. She's from Miami. She arrived at eight o'clock last night: a one night stand."

"Ever seen her before?"

For a split second, Henekey seemed to hesitate, then he shook his head.

"Not as far as I can remember. We get a lot of people here during the season. No, I guess not."

"Did she have any visitors?"

23

" I wouldn't know. I'm in this office from seven-thirty in the morning to one o'clock at night. Then I shut down and go to bed. I've no means of knowing what goes on in any of the cabins."

Terrell got to his feet.

" Let's take a look at her."

" It's cabin 24," Henekey said and put a key on the desk. " If it's all right with you, Chief, having seen her once, I don't care much to see her again."

" That's okay," Terrell said as Beigler picked up the key. The two men left the office and walked across to the double row of cabins some fifty yards ahead of them.

The group of tourists straggled after them, but came to an abrupt stop as two uniformed policemen stepped into their path. The rest of the Homicide team, with their camera man, moved from their parked cars to join Terrell and Beigler.

They arrived at Cabin 24 and Beigler unlocked the door.

" Wait here," Terrell said to his team and he and Beigler entered the cabin which was a twenty foot square room with a shabby carpet, two lounging chairs, a TV set, a hanging closet, a dressing-table and a double bed.

The stench of death made both men grimace and Beigler, after one look at the bed, went to the window and hurriedly opened it.

Terrell, his hat tilted to the back of his head, looked at the naked body lying across the bed.

Sue Parnell had been twenty-eight or nine, blonde and strikingly attractive. She must have taken good care of herself, Terrell thought, for her finger and toe nails had been recently manicured and her hair was attractively arranged. She had obviously been a sun worshipper for her body was heavily tanned.

Whoever had slaughtered her had done so with the frenzy of a madman. Four stab wounds made purple mouths in the upper part of her body. Lower down, she had been ripped. The sight of her made bile come into Terrell's mouth in spite of years of hardened experience.

Beigler said hoarsely, " For God's sake !" and feeling his

stomach begin to revolt, turned hurriedly and left the cabin.

Terrell looked around. On one of the chairs stood a blue and white suitcase. He passed the bed and opened the door leading into a tiny shower room. On the glass shelf stood a bottle of perfume, a tube of toothpaste and a tablet of soap. On another shelf by the shower was a yellow sponge and a shower cap.

He moved back into the room. Keeping his eyes away from the bed, he walked out on to the narrow veranda where his men were waiting.

" Get a sheet," he said to Hess. " Doc arrived yet?"

" He's on his way," Hess said. " Should be here any second now."

As he spoke a car pulled up and Dr. Lowis, the police M.O., came hurrying over, his bag of equipment in his hand.

" Go right on in," Terrell said. " She's all yours, and you're welcome."

Dr. Lowis, a short, fat man, gave him a questioning stare and then entered the cabin.

Terrell called his men together.

" When Doc's through, go over the place as if you're looking for a speck of dust. I want everything that can tell us anything. This is one of those jobs that has to be cleared up fast. A foot-loose sex killer usually strikes again."

He went back into the cabin and picked up the blue and white suitcase.

" Enjoying yourself?" he asked Lowis without looking at the bed.

" I've seen worse," Lowis said mildly. " Nice looking girl."

" You mean she *was* a nice looking girl," Terrell said and went out into the sunshine.

25

Chapter Three

Dr. FELIX GUSTAVE came into his waiting room where Val and her father were standing by the open french windows.

It was an impressive room. Nothing had been spared to give it an atmosphere of luxury and confidence.

Dr. Gustave was a large, heavily built man, immaculately dressed, with a bald, high dome of a head, fleshy jowls and clear, alert black eyes.

As Val and her father turned, he came across the vast room, his face expressionless as if he knew a smile wouldn't be welcomed.

"I'm sorry to have kept you waiting," he said. "Chris is in bed now." He used the Christian name without affectation. Watching him, Val felt a surge of relief that he really was on Christian name terms with her husband. "Before you see him I suggest we have a little talk about him."

Travers said sharply, "What has he been doing all the time he has been missing?"

Gustave took Val by her hand and led her to a chair.

"Let's sit down," he said, and ignoring Travers's hostility, he lowered his bulk into a chair near Val's.

Travers hesitated, then came over and sat by Val.

"You ask what he has been doing?" Gustave said. "He doesn't know. Later, he may remember, but at this moment, it is better not to ask questions. Periods of complete loss of memory are to be expected from time to time. Frankly, this nice person is for the moment very unhappy, and he has every reason to be. He has suffered serious injuries to the brain, and yet he has long periods when he is practically normal. Now this has happened, it may happen again, and he knows it."

"Is there no cure then?" Travers said impatiently. "This state of affairs has been going on for nearly two years! We thought he was showing some signs of improvement . . . now this!"

"Daddy . . . *Please!*" Val said.

Travers made an irritable movement.

"My dear, if Chris isn't going to recover, you . . ."

"A moment, Mr. Travers," Gustave said quietly. "Nothing has been said about him not making a complete recovery. This is a matter of patience." he moved slightly to look directly at Val. "While I talk to your father, you would like to see Chris, wouldn't you?"

Val nodded.

"Then go up and see him. There's a nurse in the hall. She'll take you to him. He needs affection. You are the one to give it to him."

Val got to her feet and went out into the hall. She heard a protest from her father, but she ignored it.

The elderly nurse who was waiting, took her up a flight of stairs and into a room where her husband lay in bed.

Chris Burnett was thirty-six years of age. He was a handsome man with dark hair and eyes, a firm mouth and nearly as tall as his father-in-law. Before the car crash he had been regarded by those in the know as a worthy successor to Travers's financial kingdom.

Her heart beating painfully, Val paused in the doorway.

"Chris . . . darling."

He looked up and her heart sank. His mild, indifferent expression and glazed eyes told her at once that this awful wall that had grown up between them was still there.

"Oh, hello, Val," he said. "I'm sorry about this. We don't seem to have much luck, do we?"

Val moved into the room and closed the door.

"You don't have to be sorry," she said, controlling her voice with difficulty. "Are you all right, darling?" As he said nothing, she went on, "I've been so worried."

" It only wanted this, didn't it?" he said listlessly. " Quite something to be brought to a looney-bin by two cops. Of course the real fun of it all is that I just don't know what I have been doing. I've been blacked out for hours. I could have done anything . . . murdered someone . . . anything."

" But you didn't, Chris," Val said gently as she moved to a chair by the bed and sat down. " You mustn't worry."

" That's what Gustave keeps telling me. So . . . all right . . . I'm not worrying."

She watched the nervous tick that kept twitching at the side of his mouth.

" Chris . . . do you want to come back to the hotel?"

He shook his head.

" I'm quite happy here. Gustave seems sensible. I rather like him. It would be better for me to stay here."

" I thought you liked the hotel," Val said, trying not to sound desperate. " Can't we go back there together. This . . . well, as you said, it was unlucky."

" How's your father?" Chris said, looking away from her. " I suppose he knows about this?"

Val hesitated, then said, " Oh, yes. He's downstairs talking to Dr. Gustave."

The glazed eyes moved in her direction.

" You don't mean he has dropped all his important work to come down here? How odd! He must be having a whale of a time. How he must hate me now!"

" Of course he doesn't!" Val said a little sharply. " You mustn't . . ."

" Oh, but I'm sure he does. He's as bored to death with me as I am with myself. Your father is a remarkable man, Val. He hasn't got this soft centre that I have. You know what I mean . . . a soft centre? It's something that can happen to anyone who is just ordinary. You think you are all right; that you are making a big success of life, that you have all the confidence, ambition and determination to beat the best, then suddenly the hard core that is in you . . . the hard core that you just must have if you're to get anywhere in this life . . . suddenly turns soft. That's what's

28

happened to me. It could never happen to your father. His core is made of steel."

"Please, Chris," Val said, her hands turning into fists. "You had this accident and you . . ."

"If it had happened to your father, he wouldn't be acting the way I'm acting," her husband said. "Val: I've been thinking. We'd better part. I mean this. It would be better for us both if we got a divorce and you forgot about me. I know this is what your father wants and he is absolutely right."

Val sat motionless for a long time while Chris stared impersonally at her.

"Could we wait a little while?" she said finally. "I don't want to lose you, Chris. I think if we both have patience, it'll work out."

"That reminds me," Chris said and he rubbed the back of his hand across his eyes, "I've lost that cigarette lighter you gave me. I had it with me at the hotel. I'm not all that far gone not to remember that. I had it in my jacket pocket. When the police brought me here, they tell me I wasn't wearing a jacket, so I suppose I've left it somewhere. I'm sorry about that lighter." He looked away from her. "I'm sorry about everything. You'd better not keep your father waiting. You leave me here, Val. I'll be fine. Talk to your father about a divorce. He'll fix it. There's nothing he can't fix."

"I don't want a divorce," Val said quietly. "I want to be with you always."

"That's odd . . . most girls would jump at the chance of getting rid of me. You think about it. I expect you'll change your mind. I'm sorry about the lighter. It had memories for me. I remember when you gave it to me. We were happy then, weren't we?"

"I'm still happy," Val said.

"That's fine. So long as one of us is happy. I want to sleep now. Do you mind? You talk to your father . . . he's a wonderful fixer."

He shifted further down in the bed and closed his eyes.

Val remained still, watching him. The man she was looking at wasn't the man she had married: now he was a complete stranger. After a few minutes, she saw by his regular breathing that he was asleep.

She got silently to her feet and left the room.

"Let's see what we've got," Terrell said.

He and Beigler were in one of the vacant motel cabins. On the table was the blue and white suitcase.

Latimer, one of the Homicide men, had just completed an inventory of the suitcase's contents. He stood back while Terrell and Beigler examined the various articles laid out on the table. They were few: a pair of green nylon pyjamas, stockings, underwear, a contraceptive and a green and gold embossed address book.

Terrell sat down with the address book. Beigler tossed the articles back into the case, closed it, then went out to see how the rest of the team was progressing.

Ten minutes later an ambulance arrived and two interns went into the murder cabin. They came out within a few minutes with the dead woman, covered by a sheet on a stretcher. The stretcher was loaded into the ambulance while the group of staring tourists watched from a distance. The doors were slammed and the ambulance drove rapidly away

Dr. Lowis came into the cabin where Terrell was still studying the address book.

"I'm all through," Lowis said, resting his bag on the table. "She was killed between one and three o'clock. I can't get it closer than that. She was struck on the head while taking a shower. I'd say it was a flat, heavy weapon . . . like a tyre lever. The killer dragged her from the shower and threw her on the bed. Then he stabbed her with considerable violence. She was ripped after she was dead."

"Okay, Doc," Terrell said, getting to his feet. "Let's have a detailed report as soon as you can get it on my desk. This is going to be a tricky one to solve. I'll need all the help I can get."

When Lowis had gone, Beigler came in.

"Nothing so far," as Terrell looked at him inquiringly. "These cabins get cleaned once a month by the look of them. Dozens of finger prints everywhere, but so far they don't mean a thing. Hess has got them all and he's going back to check the files. We might be lucky, but I doubt it. No sign of a weapon. The boys are making a search, but it's my bet the killer took the weapon with him. One of the occupiers of a cabin three away from the murder cabin says she heard a car arrive around one o'clock. It drove away again some twenty minutes later . . . could have been the killer."

Terrell tapped the address book.

"Lots of work here," he said. "Looks like this woman was a prostitute. The names of over two hundred men with their telephone numbers are listed in here. The only woman listed could be her sister or her mother: Joan Parnell. She lives on Le Jeune Road, near the airport. We'd better see her right away." He tossed the address book to Beigler. "I guess any one of the men listed in there could be the boy we want. It's going to be some job, but we'll have to check everyone of them. Let's go see Joan Parnell. She might give us a quick lead."

Beigler put the address book in his pocket then followed Terrell out of the cabin. Terrell had a brief word with Hess.

"See if you can get anything more out of Henekey," he said. "Keep the boys searching for the knife. Check all gas stations to see if any car stopped between one and three this morning for gas. It's pretty hopeless, but we might have a little luck. At that time, there isn't much traffic. Talk to everyone here. Get their names and addresses. We'll have to check them all . . . could be a sex killer is amongst them, but I doubt it. I'll be back at headquarters in a couple of hours. Call me if you get anything. Take your time. This one isn't going to be cracked in five minutes."

Joining Beigler, Terrell got into the police car, letting Beigler drive.

They reached Le Jeune road just after half-past two, having stopped for a few minutes at a café for a sandwich and a cup of coffee.

Joan Parnell had a neat brick and plaster bungalow that stood

31

in a row of similar bungalows. There was a tiny garden full of roses, a path that led to the front door over which climbed a flourishing Paul's Scarlet.

Leaving the car, the two men walked up the path and Beigler dug his thumb into the bell push. There was a brief delay while Terrell looked uneasily up and down the long, empty road. This distressing business of breaking the news of violent death always worried him, but it was something he never pushed onto any of his men.

The door opened abruptly and a woman regarded them. She was dark, slim, around forty with a mannish haircut and her gaunt features revealed a strength of character Terrell had seldom seen in a woman's face. She wore an open neck sports shirt and blue slacks. A cigarette dangled from her thin lips and a faint aroma of gin hung over her.

"Mrs. Parnell?" Terrell asked, lifting his hat.

"*Miss* Parnell," the woman said and looked sharply at him. "You're the police, aren't you? What is it?"

"Terrell, Chief of Police," Terrell said. "Sergeant Beigler. Could we come in?"

She gave both men another searching stare, then turned and led the way into a small lounge, comfortably furnished, but well-used. There were books everywhere, and on the table stood a bottle of Gordon's gin, a jug full of iced water and a used glass.

The woman went over to the table, poured a big shot of gin into the glass, added a little water before saying, "Well? What is it?"

"You are a relation of Sue Parnell?" Terrell asked.

She took a long thirsty drink, then hunched her shoulders.

"So that's it . . . I might have guessed. Yes, she's my sister." She looked hard at Terrell, then her mouth tightened. "Is she dead?"

Terrell drew in a breath of relief.

"I'm afraid she is, Miss Parnell."

To his surprise, she asked, "Murdered?"

"Yes."

Joan Parnell stubbed out her cigarette. She covered her eyes with her hand for a brief moment, then she stiffened, reached for the glass and finished the drink. She lit another cigarette and then walked across to a big lounging chair and sank into it.

"Sit down," she said. "Where did it happen?"

"The Park Motel at Ojus," Terrell said, sitting down near her. Beigler took a seat at the table and opened his notebook.

"I've continually warned her," the woman said in a cold, flat voice, "but that doesn't help, does it. Do you know who did it?"

"Not yet," Terrell said. "I'm hoping you could help me."

"It could be anyone. My sister led the kind of life that must eventually end in violence." Joan Parnell made an angry gesture. "People have got to work out their own destinies. She wouldn't listen to me. Well, now she's dead."

"Will you tell me about her?" Terrell asked.

"You've guessed, haven't you? She was a harlot. That's all there is to it."

"We found an address book among her possessions," Terrell said. "It contains some two hundred names. I take it, these men were her clients?"

Joan Parnell shrugged.

"How do I know? All I do know is she made a lot of money and spent a lot of money. We didn't meet very often."

"It's just possible," Terrell said, "that the dead woman might not be your sister. I'd be glad if you'd come with us and identify her."

Joan Parnell grimaced.

"I hate the sight of death. Oh, well, I'll come."

It was while they were driving to the City morgue that Terrell asked, "Did your sister have any particular boy-friend?" He was watching Joan and saw her hesitate.

"If you mean did she have a pimp, then she didn't," she said finally. "There was a man she lived with for a couple of years. She was crazy about him until he walked out on her. I had warned her about him, but she wouldn't listen . . . she never listened to me. I knew he would drop her in time."

"Who is he?"

"Lee Hardy; he's some kind of bookmaker."

Terrell and Beigler exchanged glances.

Terrell asked, "How long ago was it since he dropped her?"

"About three months. He got himself another woman. Sue went on a bender when he threw her out. She didn't sober up for three weeks."

"Would he have any reason to murder her?"

"Not unless she made a nuisance of herself. He is a man who could do anything . . . anything rotten."

Terrell absorbed this. He was still thinking about it when the car arrived at the morgue.

Minutes later they were standing behind the sheet-covered body. Beigler hovered in the background.

Carefully, Terrell turned down the sheet to reveal Sue Parnell's dead face. He looked questioningly at Joan who had lost colour.

"That's my sister," she said, her voice suddenly harsh. Before Terrell could prevent her, she caught hold of the sheet and flicked it off the naked and mutilated body. She stood as if turned to stone as Beigler hurried forward to help Terrell recover the body.

"So that's it!" she exclaimed. "I had an idea you were keeping something from me!" She turned to Terrell, her eyes blazing with a fury that startled him. "You listen to me! You find this killer! If you don't, then I will! No man is going to get away with doing that to my sister! All right, she wasn't much, but you don't do that to any woman and get away with it no matter how low she is!" She turned and ran with unsteady steps out of the morgue.

"Go after her and take her home," Terrell said. "We'll talk to her again later."

Beigler hurried after Joan. He was in time to see her get into a passing taxi. As the cab moved away, he caught a glimpse of her white gaunt face and her glittering eyes.

He went thankfully back to Terrell who was locking the door of the morgue.

"She's gone . . . took a taxi," Beigler said.

"Let's see if Hess has anything to report, then we'll talk to Hardy."

The two men walked over to where the police car was parked.

Val and her father drove back to the Spanish Bay hotel. She was tense and unhappy. She felt her father's sympathy had switched away from her while she had been with Chris and she braced herself, knowing what was coming.

It wasn't until they were back in the hotel suite that Travers said in a quietly modulated voice, "Val . . . I think you should pack right away and come back with me. I have to catch the five o'clock plane. Will you hurry? We can talk on the plane."

"I'm staying here, daddy. What should I do in New York with Chris out here?"

Her father restrained an impatient gesture.

"I've talked to Gustave," he said. "He says there is a chance of Chris *eventually* recovering, and I want you to grasp this as it is very important—in the meantime this odd blackout Chris has had makes it necessary for him to be under restraint. As he is willing to be a voluntary patient, he need not be certified, but if he shows signs of wanting to leave the sanatorium, he would have to be."

"That's all the more reason why I should stay here and see him every day," Val said steadily.

"I don't think Gustave wants you to see him every day, Val."

"He can't stop me."

Travers stared down at his well shaped hands, frowning.

"Well, Val, I suppose I'll have to tell you. Chris could become violent."

Val got to her feet and walked to the window. She stood with her back to her father. There was a long painful silence, then Travers said, "Come on, darling, get packed. Time's running out."

She turned. The determination in her eyes dismayed him.

"Did Dr. Gustave tell you that?"

"About him becoming violent? Oh, yes. If you insist on seeing Chris, you won't be able to see him alone."

"I don't understand. I've always seen him alone. Is this something new then?"

"I'm afraid so. This blackout is a warning signal. With the kind of brain injuries he has, it seems that if he has another blackout he could easily turn on anyone who is intimate with him. It's one of these odd quirks that I don't actually understand. Gustave said there could just possibly be homicidal tendencies. You couldn't stay with him or visit him without a nurse in attendance. You don't want to visit him under those conditions, do you?"

"I am going to visit him under *any* circumstances," Val said. "I am staying here."

"Poor Val! You do love him, don't you?"

"Yes, I love him. If I were in his place, I'd hope so much that he wouldn't desert me. Let's not talk about it. I am staying, daddy."

Travers got to his feet.

"Then I'll get off. I can catch an earlier plane. Keep in touch with me. I don't know what you'll do down here on your own. I don't know if you'd like one of your friends to come down and join you, but I suppose you'll manage as you always seem to manage."

"I'll be all right. I'd much sooner be on my own."

"You are never alone, Val. You have me." He looked hopefully at her. "You have, haven't you?"

"Yes, I have you," she said.

From the expression on her face, and from the tone of her voice, he realised bitterly that the hope he had had of replacing Chris, of getting her to return to his big, lonely house, of taking up their lives together once more was just bitter dust.

Lee Hardy was no stranger to the police. They knew him to be an unscrupulous gambler who ran a minor Wire Service, who managed to make a deal of money and who was shrewd enough to operate just within the law.

Terrell and Beigler called at his two room office on N.W. 17th Avenue. The pert blonde who handled the battery of telephones and ran the office when Hardy was on the race track told them that Hardy had just that moment left for home.

The two police officers went out into the hot street, climbed into the police car and drove fast to Bay Shore Drive where Hardy had a four room penthouse overlooking the Biscayne Bay.

Hardy came to the door himself. He was a tall, powerfully built hunk of beef, dark, tanned, with staring blue eyes, a dimple in his chin and would obviously be devastating to most women.

He met the hard, cold stare of the policemen with an expansive, flashing smile. He had on a red and gold patterned dressing-gown over his tanned, hairy nakedness. His feet were thrust into heel-less slippers of soft red leather.

"Chief! Well, what a surprise! Come on in. You've never visited my humble sty before, have you? Come on in . . . and you too, Sergeant."

The two men walked into a vast lounge, expensively furnished with a terrace overlooking the bay. Down one side of the room, protected by a glass screen, orchids of every colour and description grew in long, colourful ropes. The décor of the room was of white and lemon yellow. Reclining on a vast settee of yellow and white stripes was a beautifully built girl whose jet black hair reached to her golden tanned shoulders. She had on a white wrap, pulled off her shoulders and that fell away from her legs, revealing naked, tanned thighs.

Staring at her, Beigler guessed she would be around twenty-three or four. She had one of those faces that made you think of a Pekingese dog . . . attractive, but very complex.

"This is Gina Lang," Hardy said. "She takes care of my blood pressure." He gave his flashing smile. To the girl, he said "Stay right where you are, Pekie. These gentlemen are from police headquarters. Chief Terrell and Sergeant Beigler."

The girl eyed the two police officers, and then squirmed a little further down on the settee. She reached out a small, well shaped hand for a glass full of lime juice and gin. She then looked pointedly away.

"Well, gentlemen," Hardy said. "What will you drink?"

37

"You know a woman named Sue Parnell?" Terrell asked in his cop voice.

For a brief second, Hardy's smile slipped, but it was back immediately although both Terrell and Beigler had seen the question had come as a shock.

"Sue Parnell? Well, now . . . should I know her?"

Gina turned her head to stare at Hardy. Her black eyes were uncomfortably searching.

"Don't stall," Terrell snapped. "Do you know her?"

"Why, yes . . . and old, old flame that flickered out," Hardy said. "You didn't say what you would drink."

"She was murdered last night," Terrell said.

Hardy's smile slid off his face the way water leaves a sink.

"Murdered? Sue? For god's sake! Who did it?"

Neither Terrell nor Beigler were impressed with this act. They knew Hardy to be one of the trickiest punters on the Coast.

"Where were you last night?" Terrell asked as Beigler sat down and took out his notebook.

"You don't think *I* killed her, do you?" Hardy exclaimed, staring at Terrell.

"I'll ask the questions. Come on, Hardy, you're wasting time."

"Where was I last night?" Hardy said and moved to the settee. He sat down, close to Gina's naked feet. "Why . . . I was right here . . . wasn't I. Pekie?"

Gina sipped her drink. She looked at Hardy thoughtfully while Hardy stared back at her, the muscles of his neck tense.

"Were you?" She spoke with an exaggerated drawl. "Last night? How should I remember what you did last night?"

"Just think a moment," Hardy said, and Terrell saw he was controlling his temper with difficulty. "Let me remind you : we ran off that movie I made when we were down at Key West. That was around eight o'clock. I then spent an hour editing it while you listened to that new L.P. I bought you. Then we ran the movie through again. That was a little after ten o'clock. Then we played five hands of Gin and you beat me . . . remember? Then we went to bed."

38

Gina looked at Terrell, then at Beigler, then back to Hardy.

" The only thing I remember is that we went to bed," she said. " Going to bed with you is always an experience."

Hardy drew in a long deep breath. He made a helpless gesture towards Terrell.

" Pekie, this is important." There was a rasp in his voice. " Don't go vague on me. These gentlemen want to know where I was last night. I haven't any other witnesses but you. I was with you from half-past seven until this morning . . . That's right, isn't it?"

Again the long, uncomfortable pause, then Gina said, " Yes, that's right, you were. I remember now distinctly."

Hardy turned to Terrell.

" So I was here. What happened to Sue for God's sake?"

Terrell stared at Hardy. This was an alibi he disliked most . . . one he couldn't check.

" Did you have any telephone calls last night?"

" No."

" Did you go out to eat?"

" No . . . Gina fixed the meal here."

" Did anyone call on you?"

" No."

" So I have only this woman's word and yours?"

" I hope it's enough."

Terrell turned to Gina.

" If this man has had anything to do with the murder and you have lied about him being here last night, you can be charged as an accessory after the fact . . . carries quite a rap. Want to change your mind?"

Gina sipped her drink before saying, " I'm not in the habit of lying."

" Well, you have been warned," Terrell said. He nodded to Beigler and the two men walked out of the apartment.

When the front door closed behind them, Hardy said, " Thank you, Pekie, that was damn well done."

" Wasn't it?" she said and reached for a cigarette. While she lit it, he went over to the cocktail cabinet and made himself a

39

stiff whisky. As he came back and sank into a lounging chair near her, she went on, " Just who is Sue Parnell?"

" Nobody," Hardy said and switched on his flashing smile. " A tart if you're all that interested. Just nobody."

She stared at him.

" I see. Where actually were you last night, Lee?"

He made an uneasy movement.

" Pekie . . . I told you. I was out with the boys."

" Then why didn't you tell that cop?"

" He would have checked. A couple of the boys are in trouble. They wouldn't want to talk to Terrell."

" Nice friends you go around with, don't you?"

" It's business, Pekie. They aren't friends. They put business my way."

" You didn't get in until half-past three. You could have murdered this woman, couldn't you?"

" I could have, but I didn't. Let's drop it, shall we?" he said, a rasp in his voice.

" I wouldn't like you to describe me as an old, old flame that flickered out . . . a nobody . . . a tart," Gina said quietly. " I wouldn't like that at all."

" I wouldn't talk that way about you, Pekie . . . you know that."

" Well, if you did, if the flame flickered out, darling, I could always tell that cop I made a mistake in the days, and that it was Thursday and not Friday we did the things you said we did."

They stared at each other for a long moment. The hardness in her black eyes startled him and he felt a sudden sinking feeling.

" Come on, Pekie, let's drop it. Let's go to a movie or something. Look, I'll take you to the Coral Club . . . how would you like that?"

" Did you take Sue Parnell there?"

He got to his feet. Blood rushed into his face and all his smoothness went away. He looked vicious and ugly.

" Now listen, Gina . . ."

"*Pekie,* darling. You always call me that, and don't look so mad. No, we won't go to the Coral Club tonight. You run off and play with your boy-friends. I'll amuse myself on my own." She got off the settee and carrying her drink, she went across the lounge and into her bedroom.

Hardy stood motionless, his hands opening and closing, then he went into his bedroom and slammed the door.

Chapter Four

THE HARE Investigating Agency advertised that they offered superlative service with quick results.

The Agency was controlled by Homer Hare, assisted by Lucille, his daughter, and Sam Karsh, his son-in-law. They were regarded by the police and by those who had had dealings with them as " The Unholy Trinity."

Home Hare, nudging sixty-five, was an immense man, grossly fat with a turnip shaped head, a bulbous nose, shrewd little eyes and a drooping moustache that half hid a cruel, avaricious mouth.

His daughter, aged twenty-eight, was small and bony. The sharpness of her features and the brightness of her little black eyes gave her the appearance of a dangerous and suspicious ferret.

Her husband, Sam Karsh, could have been her brother. He had the same ferrety face, the same dark greasy hair and the same muddy complexion. If he hadn't been offered a job as well as a wife, it wouldn't have occurred to him to have married Lucille. He had a roving eye for any blonde who came up to his high standards, but as he made a reasonable living working with Hare, he accepted Lucille with as bad a grace as possible.

On the second morning after the murder at the Park Motel, Homer Hare sat in his specially built desk chair, designed to accept his enormous bulk, and regarded Joan Parnell with startled surprise.

"But this is a murder case," he said in his wheezy soft voice. " We don't usually take on murder cases. For one thing the police don't like an Agency to move in and for another, they have the organisation to solve a murder whereas we are necessarily handicapped."

Joan Parnell, giving off a strong aroma of gin, made an impatient movement.

"There are other Agencies," she said. "I'm not going to beg you to work for me. I'm paying a thousand dollars as a retainer. Are you taking the job or not?"

Hare blinked.

"My dear Miss Parnell," he said hurriedly, waving his great hands that looked as if they had been fashioned out of dough, "if there is one Agency that could help you, it is us. Just what do you want me to do?"

"Find my sister's killer," Joan said in her flat, hard voice.

"What makes you think the police won't find him?"

"They might, but I want the satisfaction of knowing I helped. I want this man found! Are you handling this or aren't you?"

"Of course I'll handle it," Hare said and pulled a scratch pad towards him. "I have read the facts in the papers of course, but let me see if you can tell me anything further that might help. First of all, tell me about your sister."

An hour later, Joan Parnell got to her feet. On the desk lay five hundred dollars in twenty dollar bills.

"You shall have the other five hundred next week," she said. "For this money, I want some action."

Hare regarded the money with a loving smile.

"You'll get it, Miss Parnell. We specialise in quick results. We will have something for you by next week."

"If I don't get it, you don't get any more money," Joan said curtly.

When she had gone, Hare dug an enormous thumb into a bell push on his desk.

Sam Karsh, followed by Lucille, notebook in hand, came in.

"We have a job," Hare said and pointed to the bills on the desk. "The Parnell murder."

Karsh sat down. He pushed his hat to the back of his head. He was a man who would rather go around without his trousers

43

than without his hat. There were times when he was drunk, that he went to bed with his hat on, and would turn vicious if his wife attempted to remove it.

" What's the matter with you?" he demanded. " A murder case? You gone nuts? We're in bad enough trouble with the cops as it is. You aiming to lose us our licence?"

" Relax," Hare said. " We're handling this. You leave it to me. I'll talk to Terrell. This woman has money. She's paid five hundred, and next week, she's parting with another five hundred. That's the kind of cabbage we need very, very badly."

Karsh eyed the money and grimaced.

" I don't like it. Terrell is only waiting his chance to slit our throats, but okay, so we take the job. Where does that get us? What can we do better than the cops?"

" Nothing." Hare smiled. " But we will go through the motions and we will give her an elaborate report. It will be convincing enough for us to collect the second five hundred, then we sit back and do nothing further. She'll get tired of us and go to some other Agency, but we'll have picked up a nice, easy grand."

Karsh considered this, then his ferrety face creased into a grimace he called a smile.

" Very nice . . . so what do I do?"

" You read all the newspapers covering the case. You go down to the Park Motel at Ojus and ask a few questions, then you write a report. I'll jazz it up a little and we'll present it to Miss Parnell. We'll collect the rest of the cabbage and we then can forget about her."

" I'm not poking my snout into anything until you have talked to Terrell," Karsh said firmly. " That old bull is dangerous. Once he finds out I've been poking around, he'll break my neck."

Hare reached for the telephone. A few minutes later he was speaking to Terrell.

" Chief, I've had Miss Joan Parnell here," he said, oil in his voice. " She wants to hire me to find her sister's killer."

The snap of Terrell's voice came clearly to Karsh who winced. Hare listened, breathing wheezily, then he said, " Sure, Chief, I know all that. That's why I've called you. But I won't get in your way. Sammy will be like a newspaperman. Sure, sure. I give you my word. He'll just ask a few questions here and there, then write a report. If he does come up with anything, you'll be the first to hear about it." He listened again and looked across at Karsh, lowering one fat eyelid. "All I'm trying to do, Chief, is to earn an honest buck. You can't object if Sammy goes down to the Motel and looks around. That's all he'll do." He listened again. "Okay, Chief. I give you my word. I told her we didn't take murder cases, but she wants a report . . . don't ask me why." His voice suddenly hardened. "I'm within my rights, Chief. I'll take full responsibility, and there'll be no stepping out of turn. Okay, Chief," and he hung up. He sat for some seconds staring at the telephone, then he reached for a cigar. "He can't stop us, Sammy, but watch it. He's ready to drop on us if we play it wrong.

"That's terrific," Karsh said sarcastically. "You know what? I guess I'll read all the newspapers and make a report from them. I'll stay right here in the office, then I can't go wrong."

Hare considered this, then reluctantly, he shook his head.

"She's no fool. If we're going to collect the rest of the cabbage, we'll have to do better than that. You go to the Park Motel. That's all I'm asking. See this guy Henekey: talk to one or two people there: get some local colour, then come back and we'll cook up something that will convince her."

Karsh got to his feet.

"I wonder why I ever married you," he said to his wife. "This caper could land me in jug!"

"Wouldn't I be happy!" Lucille said, her thin face lighting up. "Imagine being without you for a couple of years!"

"Now, children," Hare said disapprovingly, "that's no way to talk. You get off, Sam. See you tonight."

Karsh grunted. He made a face at Lucille who made a face back at him, then he left the office.

"I'll never know why I married that heel," Lucille said bitterly. "One of these days I'll put ground glass in his food."

Hare chuckled.

45

"Relax. He's a smart boy. We wouldn't be making much money if it wasn't for him."

"But you don't have to sleep with him," Lucille said, getting to her feet.

Hare repeated, "He's a very smart boy," and then drew some papers towards him as he re-settled his bulk in his chair.

Lucille returned to her tiny office. Sitting down in front of the typewriter, she stared moodily out of the window.

It took Tom Henekey forty-eight hours to make up his mind what to do about Lee Hardy. The reason for his long hesitation was that he was sharply aware of the danger he could walk into if he handled Hardy badly.

Hardy wasn't the kind of man anyone took liberties with. He had an organisation. He kept clear of any trouble himself, but he had been known to give the nod to Jacko Smith when some-one was being a nuisance, and that someone walked into a beat-ing that left him a hospital case.

Jacko Smith was a character who cooled angry tempers faster than any other strong-arm man on the race tracks. He was a mountain of soft white homosexual flesh with mouse-coloured hair that grew low over a narrow forehead, a fat baby face and a lisp. He went around with Moe Lincoln, a handsome, lean, vicious Jamaican who had been known to throw a knife with deadly effect at twenty yards range. Whenever there was trouble on the race tracks Jacko and Moe were there too, and the trouble lasted only for a few seconds. There was a time when these two had to resort to violence to quell trouble, but now their mere appearance had an immediate cooling effect, and they had only to stand and stare for any combatants to evaporate like ghosts. Jacko's lead pipe and Moe's knife had inflicted too many injuries for troublemakers to need further proof of their deadly efficiency.

Henekey knew he was risking a visit from these two if he needled Hardy, but after weighing the pros and the cons, he decided the pay off would be worth the risk.

So a little after eleven o'clock while he was sitting in his hot little office, he reached for the telephone and called Hardy's office.

Hardy, himself answered the call.

"This is Tom Henekey," Henekey said. "I run the Park Motel, Ojus. I'd like you to drop around here tonight: say at ten o'clock."

There was a long pause which encouraged Henekey, then Hardy said, "What's it all about?"

"This is an open line," Henekey said. "Shall we say urgent personal business?"

"If you have business with me," Hardy said, a sudden rasp in his voice, "you come to my office."

"I've had a visit from the cops," Henekey said. "They are getting nosy. I think you'd better come here and at ten o'clock." He gently replaced the receiver, marvelling at his courage to talk this way to Hardy. He took a handkerchief from his pocket and mopped his sweating face, then he opened a drawer in his desk and took from it a .38 Police Special. This he examined, satisfying himself it was loaded. He put the gun in his hip pocket.

It was while he was closing the desk drawer that his office door pushed open and a small, dark man with a ferrety face, wearing a shabby grey hat and suit, walked in.

Henekey had been vaguely aware of the sound of an arriving car. This was yet another vulture coming to see the murder cabin, he told himself, or to try to stay the night so he could boast to his friends he had slept in the same bed in which Sue Parnell had been ripped.

Ever since the murder had hit the headlines, Henekey had been pestered with these vultures. The motel was now completely full. He got to his feet to tell this little rat of a man that there were no vacancies.

"Sorry, full up," he said, scarcely bothering to look at Sam Karsh who was eyeing him narrowly. Then the light of recognition spread over Karsh's face and he sucked in his breath with excitement.

"Well, well, well! Joey Shaw of all punks! Hullo, palsy, how's the blackmail racket this year?"

Henekey froze. His sallow complexion turned grey. No one had called him Joey Shaw for the past three years. He had firmly convinced himself that he had successfully hidden his identity and got himself lost in out-of-the-way Ojus. He stared at Karsh, then his heart lurched.

Sam Karsh! *He* of all people; *Karsh* here!

Karsh's grin sent a chill down Henekey's spine.

"Are you supposed to be Tom Henekey?" Karsh asked.

Henekey hesitated, then he went slowly back to his desk and sat down.

"Hear me, palsy?" Karsh asked. He pushed his hat to the back of his head and taking out a match, he began to explore one of his side teeth.

"I'm Henekey," Henekey said huskily.

"Well, don't look so sad. Nice meeting you again. Lemme try to remember. Last time we met was around three years ago. You were operating in Key West," Karsh said. "Wonderful memory I've got, haven't I? You put the bite on a guy with more money than sense. You had a nice little puss working with you. You tucked her up in his bed and then threatened to tell his wife. You were going to take him for ten grand, only this guy wasn't so dumb as you thought he looked. He talked to Hare who talked to me, then I talked to you . . . remember?"

Henekey said, "Yes . . . that's right."

"We had to get a little rough with you. You signed a statement . . . remember? We even managed to persuade you to sign two other statements concerning two other more successful blackmail attempts. We said we would hold all these statements so long as you behaved yourself. By the way, what happened to the puss? I could have gone for her myself."

"I don't remember," Henekey said huskily.

"Pity . . . well, I guess there are other pussies around," Karsh said. "The cops know who you are, Joey?"

"Don't call me that!" Henekey exclaimed.

"So they don't know . . . very, very interesting." Karsh came around the counter and sat in the chair opposite Henekey. "Well, now what do you know about the Parnell killing, Joey?

48

I'm working on the case. You give me something and I'll give you something . . . *quid pro quo* as they say in the classics. What's the inside dirt?"

Henekey relaxed a little in his chair.

"The cops have it all. You can read about it in the papers. She came here, booked in, put in an early call . . ."

"I know all that crap," Karsh said. "I want the meat of it, Joey. The stuff you didn't spill to the cops."

"There was nothing to spill," Henekey said, sweat breaking out on his face.

"But I have something to spill, Karsh said. "*Quid pro quo,* Joey."

"I tell you there's nothing to spill," Henekey said desperately. "Look, Karsh, I'm going straight. I can't help it if some tart gets knocked off in my motel, can I? Give me a break. If there was something, I'd tell you."

Karsh stared at him for a long moment, then he shrugged and got to his feet.

"I don't mind crooks, thieves, killers or con men. I can even stomach a pimp now and then, but I just can't live alongside a blackmailer. Palsy, in a little while, you're going to have a load of law in your lap and they'll be clutching in their big sweaty hands the statement you signed three years ago."

Henekey who had been in many tough jams before, thought quickly. He knew if Karsh betrayed him to the police, Terrell would be on his neck long before ten o'clock when Hardy was due to arrive. Somehow he had to stall Karsh, get at Hardy, raise a get-away stake and disappear once more.

Karsh was drifting to the door when Henekey said, "Wait . . ."

Karsh paused.

"Give me a break," Henekey said urgently. "If I knew something, I'd tell you. I don't even know who the woman was."

"Yeah?" Karsh sneered and reached the door. "This is your last chance, Joey. Spill something or stand by for the sirens."

Henekey appeared to hesitate, then he reached into his pocket and took out a small object which he laid on the desk.

49

"Okay, you win. There it is. I swear that's all I've been holding back. I found it by the dead woman's body."

Karsh who had been bluffing and hadn't expected to gain anything from his threats, walked to the desk and regarded the solid gold cigarette lighter that Henekey was offering him. He didn't touch it, but he examined it closely. This was a costly item, he told himself. He looked searchingly at Henekey.

"When I found her," Henekey explained, "I was so fazed, I didn't know what I was doing. I saw this lighter right by her on the bed and I picked it up and put it in my pocket. I forgot about it when I talked to the cops."

"Yeah?" Karsh sneered. "You think I have a hole in my head? You saw it and you couldn't resist stealing it." He picked up the lighter and examined it more closely, then he turned it and his eyes narrowed as he read the engraved inscription on the back of the lighter:

Chris—with love—Val.

"Who is Chris and who is Val?
Henekey shook his head.

"I wouldn't know. I got the idea this belonged to the killer. Why should it belong to the Parnell woman?"

"She could have stolen it," Karsh said, but he didn't sound convinced.

"That's all I can give out," Henekey said. "Honest, Karsh, I wouldn't lie to you."

Karsh didn't seem to be listening. He continued to examine the lighter, then after a long moment of hesitation, he dropped the lighter into his pocket.

"Okay, Joey, *quid pro quo.* I'll keep my mouth shut and you keep yours shut. I could be seeing you again so don't hang out the bunting just yet."

He walked out of the office, and Henekey, his face tense, watched him drive rapidly away in a dusty aged Buick.

Karsh stopped off at the Ojus Post Office. He put through a

call to the office. When Hare came on the line, Karsh told him about Henekey and the lighter.

"What do you want me to do?" he asked at the end of his recital. "Give the lighter to the cops?"

"We mustn't rush anything," Hare wheezed. "Never rush anything, Sammy. Chris and Val you say? Now why should those two names ring a bell in my mind? I want a little time to think. You go and have a nice cold beer. Telephone me in about an hour. I've got thinking to do."

After he had hung up he sat for some minutes, his fat face tight with concentration, then he reached out and rang for Lucille.

"Get me a copy of the *Miami Herald* for yesterday," he said as she poked her head around the door. "Fast, honey."

When she had brought him a paper he waved her away. He flicked through the pages until he came to the Society Gossip column where he read that Charles Travers, the tenth richest man in America had flown out from New York to spend a couple of days with his daughter and son-in-law, Chris Burnett. Further down the column, he learned that Mrs. Burnett's Christian name was Valerie. He also learned the young couple were staying at the Spanish Bay hotel. He then called for this morning's edition of the *Miami Herald*. He learned of Chris's disappearance and re-appearance, but the information was so slight he was unable to form an opinion of what had actually happened to Burnett. He put a call through to the Spanish Bay hotel and asked to speak to Henry Trasse, the hotel detective who was on Hare's payroll. He listened to what Trasse had to tell him about the Burnetts, grunted and hung up. He then lit a cigar and sat slumped into his chair for some time while his evil, fertile mind was busy. It was only when Karsh telephoned that he came alive.

"Sammy, I think we are onto something very, very interesting. The lighter belongs to Chris Burnett, the son-in-law of Charles Travers . . . yeah . . . that's the one. Trasse tells me Burnett is a nut. A couple of days ago, he took off from his hotel and was absent for twenty-four hours or so. He was picked up by the cops. He didn't know what he had been doing or where he had been. He's in Gustave's squirrel farm right now. Now look, Sammy, this could be a very profitable deal if we play our hand right. Here's what I want you to do. I want you to drive from the Park Motel towards the North Miami Beach highway. All along the route taking your time, I want you to keep your eyes skinned. Check all the dirt roads. Burnett must have had a car. He was also wearing a sports jacket when he left the hotel. It was missing when the cops found him. If you could find the jacket, we would be sitting very pretty. Work at it, Sammy. Pull out all the stops in your organ. I want the full bloodhound treatment."

Karsh cursed under his breath as he sweated in the hotel telephone booth.

"You want me to turn the lighter over to Terrell?" he asked.

"No more than I want you to cut my heart out and drop it in the harbour," Hare returned.

"Who said you had a heart?" Karsh snarled and hung up.

Leaving the booth, he got into his car. He lit a cigarette, tipped his hat over his eyes and sat for some moments, thinking. When Hare had said he wanted the bloodhound treatment he was referring to Karsh's uncanny knack of discovering the undiscoverable. It was almost as if Karsh was psychic. Time after time he had been able to solve a case simply because he had this odd feeling that he would find the necessary clue if he looked in a particular place. He looked and he found it.

While he sat smoking, he completely relaxed, his eyes closed, his ferrety face in repose, then after some minutes, he straightened his hat, started the car and drove rapidly back to the Park Motel. At the entrance of the motel, he U-turned and then started to drive towards the North Miami Beach highway, some fifty miles ahead of him.

He drove at a steady thirty miles an hour and his mind was like an antenna, groping for something that would home him onto the thing he sought.

It was growing dusk when he was within three miles of where Burnett had been found. He had explored every side road, reversing when he had found nothing and returning to the highway. Now, he suddenly became alert. A dirt track to his right led off the highway and into the dense woodland. It was more of a cart track than a road and Karsh had no hesitation in turning his car up the track, and as the car bumped over the uneven surface, he began to whistle under his breath. He had this sudden strong feeling that he was about to find what he was looking for.

Halfway up the track he came to a small clearing in heavy forest land. On the clearing stood a white and blue Ford Lincoln. It had a deserted appearance and he stopped his car, got out and walked over to the Lincoln.

He wandered around the car, inspecting it closely, then he took from his hip pocket a pair of well-used pigskin gloves which he put on. Then he opened the driver's door and slid under the wheel. He examined the licence tag hanging from the steering column. He learned the car was owned by U-Drive Car Hire Service, Miami. He turned around and looked on the back seat. On the seat, neatly folded, inside out, was a man's sports jacket. Still whistling, Karsh lifted the jacket and laid it across his knees. In the inside pocket was a slim, expensive-looking wallet. This he examined. It contained two fifty dollar bills and three one hundred dollar bills, a driving licence made out in the name of Chris Burnett of New York, and a snapshot of a nice-looking girl in a smart swim suit. On the back of the snap shot, scrawled in pencil was the one word : " Val."

When Karsh unfolded the coat he got a shock that abruptly stopped his whistling. The front of the coat was heavily encrusted with dried blood. Karsh was too old a hand not to recognise the rust-like stains. He sat for some moments staring at the coat, feeling sweat gathering on his low forehead, then he hurriedly refolded the coat and getting out of the car, he went over to his car and locked the jacket in his boot. He returned to the Lincoln and although he spent twenty minutes going carefully over every inch of the car, he found nothing else. By now it was seven-twenty-five o'clock and getting dark. He returned to his car, lit a cigarette, brooded for about three minutes, then U-turned and drove back to the highway. He reached Miami a little after eight-thirty, having driven fast and carefully, his mind busy.

He decided to call on the U-Drive Car Hire Service before contacting Hare. From long experience, he knew Hare never thanked him for coming up with only half the information necessary to swing into action.

The manager of the U-Drive Hire Service was a willowy blond man with heavy bags under his eyes and a frown of perpetual worry creasing his forehead.

Karsh gave him his business card and then draped his small frame into a chair.

" Came across one of your cars," he said. " Seems abandoned. Licence No. 44791. Mean anything to you?"

The manager whose name was Morphy, frowned at him.

"Abandoned . . . what do you mean?"

" Up a dirt road off the North Miami Beach highway," Karsh explained. " Dumped in a wood clearing . . . no driver . . . no nothing. I thought you might be glad to know."

Morphy reached for his register. He thumbed through the pages, found an entry, read it, frowned some more and then sat back.

" I don't understand. We hired the car to Miss Ann Lucas for five days. Maybe she was taking a walk in the woods or something."

"You got a map of the district?" Karsh asked.

Morphy produced a map from his desk drawer. Karsh examined it, then marked the map with a pen.

"That's where the car is. If after five days you don't get it back . . . that's where you'll find it."

Morphy seemed to be getting uneasy.

"You don't think she was taking a walk or something?"

" I wouldn't know. I get hunches. I got the idea the car's been dumped. Who is Ann Lucas anyway?"

Morphy consulted his register.

" She lives at 237, Coral Avenue. Never seen her before. I checked her driving licence. She paid the usual deposit. I even checked her in the phone book."

" You remember what she looked like?"

" Sure. A blond: well dressed. She had on a head scarf and sun goggles: around twenty-five . . . why?"

" Know her again?"

" Why, sure."

" Without the head scarf and goggles?"

Morphy stared at him uneasily.

" Well, no . . . I didn't see much of her. What's all this about?"

Karsh got to his feet.

" Force of habit, palsy," he said. " When talking to me, you have to expect questions like that." He showed his yellow teeth in what he called a smile. " Well, you know where your car is if you want it. So long," and he walked back to his car.

He drove to a drug store and shutting himself in a sweltering telephone booth, he looked up Ann Lucas in the book. He found her number and dialled. While he waited for the connection, he looked at his strap watch. The time was half-past nine.

There was a click and then a girl's voice said, " Hello?"

Miss Lucas?"

" That's right."

" You own a driving licence No. 559700. That right?"

" I don't know the number, but I have lost my driving licence. Have you found it?"

" How did you lose it?"

" Someone stole my bag."

" Did you report the loss?"

" Of course I did. I reported it to the police a couple of days ago. Who is this talking?"

" Did you hire a U-Drive car a couple of nights ago?"

" Why, no. Who is this . . . is it the police?"

" Could be," Karsh said. " Could be anyone," and he hung up. He left the booth and drove fast to the office.

Homer Hare was unwrapping a large parcel containing thickly cut beef sandwiches.

" Just what I was hoping to find," Karsh said, scooping up two of the sandwiches. These he carried with him to a chair opposite

55

Hare's desk. Hare sighed and looked at Lucille. " Tell the boy to bring some more and another carton of coffee."

Karsh ate hungrily. When he had wolfed the sandwiches he looked expectantly at the pile before Hare, but Hare covered them with his arm. " You wait . . . these are mine." Karsh made a grab for the carton of coffee, but Hare was too quick for him.

" Mine too," Hare said shoving Karsh's hand away.

" What a hog l" Karsh said bitterly. " While I'm earning the money, you just sit here and stuff your cave."

Lucille came in with more sandwiches and a carton of coffee. As soon as Karsh started eating again, he said, his mouth full, " Is this Burnett really a nut?"

" No doubt about it," Hare said, his mouth equally full. " He got into a car smash a couple of years ago and he's been a scrambled brain ever since."

Karsh poured coffee, finished his sandwich, then recited the events of the afternoon and evening. Long before he had finished, Hare had stopped eating and was listening intently, his little eyes glazed with concentration.

" Looks for sure this nut killed the woman," Karsh said. " His lighter was on the bed and his jacket covered with blood. This is going to make Terrell look as high as an ant."

" The car puzzles me," Hare said, lifting the last of the sandwiches from the wrapping. " Who was the woman who hired the car? You don't think it was Ann Lucas?"

" No, but we can check. I think some woman stole her bag and used her licence to hire this car. Why? How did Burnett's coat get into the car? You know with what we've got, we could put the bite on Joan Parnell for a lot more than a thousand bucks."

" We're wasting time," Lucille broke in. " Terrell won't like this delay. Sam should have gone straight to headquarters, reported finding the car, the lighter and the jacket."

" I was going to do just that," Karsh said irritably, " but Big-Brain here said not." He looked at Hare. " You want to go to headquarters in person, is that the idea?"

Hare licked his great, thick fingers, peered into the wrapping to make sure he hadn't left anything he could eat, then regretfully screwed up the paper and dropped it into his trash basket. He then lit a cigar and blew smoke up to the ceiling.

"No, that's not the idea, Sammy," he said. "I've been giving this affair considerable thought. Handled properly it could be very, very profitable."

"I heard you the first time," Karsh said staring at him. "So we up the price to the Parnell woman : what would she stand for?"

"We don't do that," Hare said. Absently, he reached for Karsh's last sandwich, but Karsh was too quick for him. "I didn't think you wanted it," Hare said in a hurt voice.

"I do . . . keep talking."

Hare sighed and folded his hands over his enormous stomach.

"Tomorrow morning, Lucille will take the five-hundred dollars the Parnell woman paid us and she'll call on her. She'll tell her we can't take the assignment. She'll explain that I have talked to Terrell and he is against a private agency moving in on a murder case. Lucille will then give her back the money and duck out."

Karsh stared at Hare as if he thought he had gone out of his mind.

"He's been eating too much," he said to his wife. "His brains are clogged with food."

Lucille said, "From where then do we make our very interesting profit?"

Hare smiled at her.

"From Valerie Burnett . . . who else?"

Karsh sat bolt upright in his chair. His ferrety face became tense.

"Now wait a minute . . ."

Hare stopped him by raising his big doughy hand.

"This is the chance of a lifetime, Sammy. The Burnetts have money, and Travers is worth millions. Do you imagine he would want his son-in-law to stand trial for murder? Do you imagine Travers would allow his son-in-law to spend the rest of his days in a Criminal Asylum?"

Karsh shifted uneasily.

"While we are asking questions," he said, "have you ever heard of a little word called 'blackmail'? Have you any idea what kind of rap blackmail draws?"

"Have you ever heard of half a million dollars?" Hare said, hunching his massive shoulders and staring at Karsh. "Travers will jump at the chance of buying the lighter and the jacket for half a million. You see . . . I'll handle it. You leave this to me."

"Not me." Karsh got to his feet. "Oh no. I'm getting along pretty well as I am. I'm not going to be locked up in a cell for fourteen years just to please you."

"You won't be pleasing me," Hare said quietly. "You will be on the receiving end of half a half a million dollars."

Karsh started for the door, paused, then came slowly back to his chair.

"You really think you can swing it?"

"I know I can. Think about it, Sammy. So far the cops haven't an idea it is Burnett. With the evidence we have got, he hasn't got a prayer. He'll be put away in a squirrel house for life. Travers would pay more than half a million dollars to avoid that. You leave it to me, Sammy. You've done your share, now I'll do mine, and we split the take."

"Don't I get in on the split?" Lucille asked, her thin face ugly with greed.

Karsh glared at her.

"You're my wife . . . remember?"

"It'll be split three ways," Lucille said, "or it doesn't get split at all."

The two men stared at her, then Hare, who knew his daughter, said with a resigned sigh, "So it'll be split three ways."

Chapter Five

LEE HARDY slowed his Cadillac when he came in sight of the entrance to the Park Motel. Pulling into a lay-by, he stopped the car.

"Okay, boys, stick around, but keep out of sight," he said. "I may not need you, but it's my guess I will."

Jacko Smith belched gently as he heaved his gross body out of the car. Moe Lincoln, smelling of a new perfume Jacko had given him, slid out after him.

"Enjoy the moon," Hardy said. "You don't do a thing until I give you the nod."

"That's fine with us, dear," Jacko said. "We'll be right here if you want us."

Leaving them, Hardy drove on towards the motel. The time was five minutes after ten and he found Henekey waiting for him. As Hardy walked into the stuffy little office, Henekey who had seen him park his car, was standing by his desk.

"Come on in, Mr. Hardy," Henekey said. "Glad you could come."

Hardy walked across to the chair opposite Henekey's desk and sat down.

"You said urgent personal business," he said, his voice harsh. "I hope for your sake you haven't brought me here on a bum steer. What is it?"

Henekey sat down. His heart was thumping, and there was a film of sweat on his face.

"Something I thought we should talk over together, Mr.

Hardy. Something you wouldn't want to discuss over an open line."

" What is it?" Hardy repeated.

" Sue Parnell," Henekey said. His eyes went past Hardy to the window and then to the door. His hand, now behind him, rested on the butt of his gun.

" She's nothing to me," Hardy said.

Henekey hesitated, then he forced a smile.

" Well, that's fine. Then what she told me must have been all lies. Okay, then I'm very sorry, Mr. Hardy, I've given you this trip for nothing. I can now go and talk to Terrell."

The two men stared at each other, then Hardy rubbed his hand over his smooth, closely shaven chin.

" You could be talking yourself into trouble," he said, a rasp in his voice.

" Not me," Hardy said with more confidence than he felt. " I'm old enough to take care of myself. I had the idea Sue Parnell did mean something to you, that's why I didn't talk to the cops. I thought we might do a deal. But if she doesn't mean anything to you, then I still have time to talk to Terrell without getting into trouble."

" Just what are you getting at?" Hardy demanded, sitting forward.

" I've known Sue now for more than two years," Henekey said. " We had a business arrangement. Whenever she had a business date she didn't want to take to her home she came here. Sure, I could get into trouble . . . immoral earnings and all that, but I reckon Terrell would forget about that if I told him about you."

Hardy drew in a whistling breath.

" And what would you tell him?"

" What Sue told me," Henekey said. He kept looking to the window and the door. He was scared that at any moment Jacko Smith and his boy friend might walk in. He gripped the butt of his gun so tightly his fingers began to ache.

" What did Sue tell you?" Hardy asked.

" That she was blackmailing you. Maybe she was lying . . . I wouldn't know, but she said she had enough on you to put you away for ten years and she was shaking you down. She came here the night she died and told me she was expecting you. You were paying her five thousand dollars for her to keep her mouth shut. She was scared of you. She asked me to watch her cabin. Unless I was drunk or dreaming, I was under the impression you arrived around one o'clock. You left around one-thirty. As I say, I could have imagined it, but I have this very strong impression."

"You're crazy!" Hardy snarled, his eyes gleaming with suppressed rage. "I was nowhere near this dump!"

Henekey shrugged.

"Well, there you are, Mr. Hardy, so I was dreaming. So Sue was lying."

Hardy got to his feet.

"Now listen, Henekey, I'm warning you. You say one word of this to the police and you'll get it. I mean that! I was at home when that tart was knocked off and I can prove it. You lay off or you'll be as good as dead!"

"I'm listening, Mr. Hardy," Henekey said, "but Sue trusted me. She gave me an envelope she stole from your safe. I have it in my bank. Even if the cops can't pin her murder on you, once they look inside that envelope they could put you away for years."

Hardy stood motionless for a long moment, then he sat down.

"You have the envelope?"

"Right in my bank, Mr. Hardy, with instructions that if anything happens to me, it goes to the cops."

"What happened to the five thousand dollars I gave that bitch?"

Henekey shrugged.

"I wouldn't know, Mr. Hardy. Maybe the cops took it . . you know cops."

"Know what I think? I think after I left her, you went into her cabin, murdered her and took the five grand. That's a theory Terrell would like to explore."

" That's right," Henekey smiled. " He could make it tricky for me, but he could make it much more tricky for you. I'm willing to take the risk : are you?"

Hardy thought for a moment, rubbing his chin, then he shrugged.

" Okay, you creep, how much?"

Henekey took his aching fingers off the butt of his gun.

" I'm in trouble too, Mr. Hardy. People are crowding me. I want to get away. I want to get lost . . . "

" How much?" Hardy snarled.

" Five grand, and I'll turn the envelope over to you, drop out of sight and you'll never hear from me again."

Hardy took a pack of cigarettes from his shirt pocket. He flicked out a cigarette and set fire to it.

" Okay, it's a deal," he said. " Get the envelope and I'll be back tomorrow morning with five grand."

" Back *alone*, Mr. Hardy," Henekey said. " We'll meet right here in this office. If anything should happen to me between then and now my bank have their instructions.

" You told me. I know when I have to lose money and when I don't. You'll get paid, creep, but get out of sight fast. If ever Jacko runs into you after I've paid you, I'm not responsible."

Henekey took the gun from his hip pocket ad laid it on the table.

" Just for the record, Mr. Hardy, I won't be responsible for Jacko either."

Hardy stared at him, then he got to his feet.

" Around eleven tomorrow morning," he said, " but don't imagine you're going to put the bite on me again. It's five grand and no more."

" All I want is a getaway stake," Henekey said and for the first time since Hardy had walked into his office, he began to relax. " There'll be no second bite."

Hardy walked out, crossed the lighted car park and got into his car. Strident swing music came from the loudspeakers, hanging in the trees. The fairy lights strung across the cabins flickered with pseudo prettiness. Henekey, breathing heavily, his hand still on his gun, watched Hardy go.

Hardy pulled into the lay-by where Jacko and Moe were waiting. He got out of the car and joined them on the grass verge.

"It's a shake-down," he said as he flicked his half smoked cigarette into the darkness. "He's got enough on me to get me ten years. It's up to you two. He says he's put the evidence in his bank with instructions for it to be handed to the police if anything happens to him. He's bluffing. I want you two to soften him and get the stuff from him. This is important to me. It's worth a grand."

Moe stretched his elegant long arms and smiled happily.

"Man. It's a long time since I've worked a jerk over. It'll be a pleasure, Mr. Hardy."

Hardy looked at Jacko who sat in a massive heap of fat on the grass.

"We'll fix him, dear," Jacko said, "but what do we do with the creep after we've got what you want?"

"He's best out of the way, Jacko."

"Moe keeps on at me for a new car. I don't know where he thinks the money is to come from. Could you make it two grand, dear, and we'll make a very nice job of it for you."

"Two grand it is," Hardy said without hesitation. "Watch it . . . he has a gun."

Moe got to his feet. He capered in front of Jacko who watched him admiringly. He turned a couple of handsprings, then thrust out a lean, brown hand to help Jacko lever himself to his feet.

"Better wait until the joint shuts down," Hardy said. "You two go ahead and find out where he sleeps. Wait for him there. I'll stay here. Remember the gun." As they began to move off, Hardy said, "There's five grand he took from Sue Parnell. I want that too."

It was a little after one o'clock when Henekey switched off the flashing neon sign. By then most of the cabins were in darkness. He locked up his office and stepped into the hot night air.

Although he was pretty sure he had thrown a scare into Hardy, he was very cautious. He held the gun in his hand and he looked carefully over the moonlit space that separated him from his cabin. There were still a few people sitting on their porches, enjoying the moonlight, talking together and having the last cigarette before going to bed. Their presence gave Henekey confidence.

He walked slowly from his office, pausing now and then to have a word with the people outside their cabins until he finally reached his own cabin. It was a hot night and Henekey's mind was too active for immediate sleep. He sat down in the basket chair on the porch and lit a cigarette. This time tomorrow, he thought he would have ten thousand dollars : five he had stolen from Sue Parnell and five he would be getting from Hardy. With that kind of money, he would fly to New York and get lost. It was time he left Miami. He sat for some thirty minutes trying to make up his mind what he would do in New York. He had never been good at making plans. Maybe it would be better to wait until he got to New York, he thought. He looked at his watch. It was now twenty minutes to two. He stifled a yawn. The rest of the cabins were now in darkness. Time to turn in. By now Hardy would be back in Miami. Henekey decided he had nothing to worry about from Hardy. He would be smart enough to know when he was licked. He got to his feet, stretched, then opening his cabin door, he walked into the hot, stuffy darkness.

As he groped for the light switch, a hard, perfumed hand closed over his nose and mouth and what felt like the hoof of a horse slammed into his stomach.

Moe found the loose tile in the bathroom. He lifted it, put his hand into the cavity and drew out a sealed envelope. He groped again and came up with a thick bundle of dollar bills. He replaced the tile and returned to the sitting-room.

Jacko was slumped in a chair, mopping the sweat off his face. Henekey lay on the settee, moaning faintly from behind the gag that half suffocated him.

"Got it, honey?" Jacko asked.

Moe handed him the envelope and the money. The two glanced at Henekey and then at each other.

"Take it to Mr. Hardy. Find out if it's what he wants," Jacko said. He took a carton of chocolate from his pocket and fed a chocolate into his small, wet mouth.

Moe slid away into the darkness. Running lightly and swiftly, he reached Hardy who was waiting in the Cadillac.

"Good God!" Hardy snarled. "You've taken your time! It's nearly four o'clock."

Moe smiled his beautiful, evil smile.

"The creep was a little obstinate," he said. "He really did resist. Is this what you want, Mr. Hardy?"

Hardy took the money and the envelope. He broke the seals and went quickly through the contents.

"Yeah . . ."

He got out of the car, took out his cigarette lighter and set fire to the papers. As he watched them burn, he asked, "What's happened to Henekey?"

Moe showed his magnificent teeth in a flashing smile.

"Right now he seems pretty sick, Mr. Hardy. He seems awful unhappy. I'll go back now and we'll make him happy."

Hardy felt a sudden tightening in his throat. He had never told those two to commit murder before. They were like trained animals. They would do just what he told them to do. He hesitated, then he reminded himself that he could never really be safe as long as Henekey was alive.

"What the hell are you hanging around me for like a grinning ape?" he snarled. "Get back to Jacko."

Moe executed a neat handspring, then darted away into the darkness.

Jacko was eating his sixth chocolate when Moe slipped into the cabin.

"It's okay," Moe said quickly. "Mr. Hardy has what he wants."

Jacko wiped his sticky fingers on his handkerchief. Still munching, he levered himself out of his chair.

65

" We'll put the creep out of his misery," he said. " I want to
go to bed."

The two men, one vast and gross, the other perfumed and
slim, walked over to where Henekey lay. Moe leaned over and
patted his face.

" You're a brave jerk, jerk," he said. " So long and sweet repose."

Henekey looked up at him indifferently. His body raved with
pain. He was ready to die.

With a flourish, Moe picked up a cushion lying in one of the
chairs and laid it across Henekey's face, then he bowed to
Jacko.

" You may be seated you great big beautiful doll," he said.

Jacko moved his enormous body to the settee and, after hitch-
ing up his trousers, he lowered his vast buttocks down onto the
cushion.

Homer Hare was at his desk early the following morning. He
put a call through to the Spanish Bay hotel and spoke to Trasse,
the hotel detective.

" I want to talk to Mrs. Burnett in private," Hare said, wheezing into the telephone mouthpiece. " I don't imagine she would
see me if I sent my card up. What do I do?"

" What's the matter with the beach?" Trasse asked after a
moment's thought. " She's on the beach every morning between
ten and twelve. You get here around ten and I'll point her out
to you. What's it all about?"

" I'll be there ten minutes after ten," Hare said and hung up.

He went over to the safe, opened it and took from it Chris
Burnett's jacket and cigarette lighter. He put the lighter in his
pocket and laid the jacket on the desk. He rang for Lucille. She
came in and looked inquiringly at him.

" Be a nice girl and make a parcel of this jacket for me," Hare
said.

Lucille eyed the jacket and then looked again at her
father.

" Are you sure you know what you are doing?" she asked.

66

" I don't like this a lot. From what I read in the papers, Travers is a tough cookie and he plays it rough."

Hare beamed on her.

" Don't worry your head about him," he said. " I'll talk to his daughter first. If anyone can persuade him to part with half a million, she can."

Lucille shrugged uneasily.

" Well, all right, but don't forget I warned you." She picked up the jacket with a grimace and took it away.

Hare lit a cigar and lowered his bulk into the desk chair. He stared through the window, frowning. It was a risk, he thought, but to make a killing of half a million dollars was something he couldn't resist. But he must be careful how he handled Mrs. Burnett. He had to be ready to bow out at the slightest sign of danger.

Ten minutes later, he clapped his yellow panama hat on his head, picked up the brown paper parcel Lucille had put on his desk and walked slowly and heavily to the elevator. Out on the street he climbed into the office car and drove towards the Spanish Bay hotel.

He found Trasse, a thickset florid faced ex-cop waiting for him. The two men walked down the flower lined path that led to the private beach.

" If anyone finds out I fingered Mrs. Burnett for you," Trasse growled, " I would lose my job. What's the idea anyway?"

" I want to talk to her," Hare wheezed. " Phew! I'm not as young as I used to be. Don't walk so fast."

" The trouble with you is you eat too much," Trasse said, slowing his pace. " What do you want to talk to her about?"

" Private business, Henry. Nothing that would interest you."

Trasse looked suspiciously at him, then paused as they came in sight of the beach and the sea. It was still early, and there were very few people lying about on the sand.

Trasse pointed to a distant figure, sitting under a sun umbrella.

" There she is. Don't blame me if you get thrown out. If she yells for help, I'll be the one to do the throwing."

"She won't yell," Hare said. "Put twenty bucks on your next expense sheet, Henry," and tucking the brown paper parcel more firmly under his arm, he set off slowly across the sand towards where Val was sitting.

Val was feeling depressed. She had talked to Dr. Gustave on the telephone before coming down to the beach and he had said he had found Chris less well.

"There's nothing to worry about," he had assured her. "One must expect off days. He seems to have something on his mind. I think it would be a good idea if you came out here this afternoon. He might talk to you."

Val said she would come.

"Be quite natural. Tell him what you have been doing," Gustave went on. "Don't ask questions. There's a chance he might unburden to you."

After this conversation, she had to make an effort to go down to the beach, but now she was there, she was pleased. It was quiet, and she could relax a little in the warmth of the sun.

She glanced around and saw this enormous old man wearing a wrinked white tropical suit and an ageing panama hat plodding towards her. She wondered who he was, and suddenly she realised he was heading her way. She looked quickly away. Opening her beach bag, she took out a pack of cigarettes.

The old man was very close to her now, and as she tapped out a cigarette, he said, "Allow me, madam." He raised his hat with a little flourish and flicked a flame to the gold cigarette lighter he held in his enormous hand.

Val looked around.

"Thank you, but it is quite all right."

As she was about to turn her back, her eyes fell on the lighter. She felt her heart skip a beat, making her catch her breath sharply.

"Sorry to have disturbed you, madam," Hare wheezed. "An old man's weakness. These days it seems chivalry is out of date." He snapped the light shut while his beady little eyes watched Val's reactions. He saw her hesitate, then he deliberately dropped the lighter into his pocket. He lifted his hat and then turned and began to move slowly away.

"Wait . . ." Val got to her feet. She was wearing pale blue beach pyjamas, and she looked slim and lovely as she moved out of the umbrella's shade into the sunlight.

Hare paused. They faced each other.

"That lighter . . . I think I've seen it before," Val said unsteadily. "May I see it?"

"Why certainly madam," Hare said. He came close to her. She could feel the heat coming from his vast body and she could hear the wheezing of his breathing. "This lighter?" He took the lighter from his pocket, turned it so the inscription showed and held it out to her.

Val stared at the lighter, then she looked sharply at Hare.

"I don't understand," she said. "This belongs to my husband. Where did you get it from?"

Hare studied the lighter as if he had never seen it before then he walked heavily to the shade of the umbrella. With a stifled grunt, he lowered himself down on the sand.

"It is some time since I have been on a beach," he said, staring across the wide expanse of sand. "It's very pleasant. My wife, who has been dead now for some years, used to be a beach lover."

Val stared down at the top of the yellow panama hat, her heart beating rapidly. There was something about this gross old man that frightened her.

"I asked you where you got that lighter," she said in a tight, strained voice.

"The lighter? Oh, I found it." Hare tilted his head so he could look up at her. "Won't you sit down, madam?"

"Where did you find it?" Val demanded, not moving.

"So it belongs to your husband," Hare said musingly. "How is he today?"

"Will you please tell me where you found it?"

"Dear madam, don't be impatient with a feeble old man," Hare said. "Do please sit down. You wouldn't force such a heavy old fellow like myself to remain on his feet, would you?"

69

Val dropped onto her knees. She felt something bad was coming. She could tell by the sly, simpering smile and the beady staring eyes that this dreadful old man wouldn't be hurried.

There was a long pause, then Hare said, "You are Mrs. Christopher Burnett?"

"Yes."

"I understand your husband is in a sanatorium?"

Val's hands turned into fists, but she managed to control herself to say, "Yes."

"He disappeared from the hotel a couple of days ago and was found by two policemen?"

"All this was reported by the newspapers," Val said. "What is it to you?"

Hare lifted a fistful of sand and let it run through his fat fingers.

"I don't wonder that children love to play on a beach," he said and chuckled. "Perhaps I'm getting senile. I wouldn't mind having a bucket and spade right now."

Val said nothing. She regarded him with growing horror.

"It seems Mr. Burnett had a black-out," Hare continued after a long pause, "and he has no idea what he did during the night of the 18th."

Val felt a cold shiver run down her spine. There now seemed no heat in the sun.

"This must be very worrying to you, madam," Hare went on and gave his sly little smile. "Even when wives have normal husbands, they worry when they don't know where they have been, but when they have abnormal husbands, the worry is even greater."

Val said, "Just what do you want? I'm not going to listen to you much longer. What is it? Where did you get that lighter?"

Hare took from his billfold a newspaper cutting.

"I would be glad if you would glance at this madam," he said, offering the cutting.

Val took it suspiciously. It was a brief account of the finding of Sue Parnell's body at the Park Motel, Ojus with an interview with Police Chief Terrell who said it was obvious that the killer was a sexual sadist.

Val let the cutting flutter from her cold fingers.

" I don't understand," she said.

Hare took the lighter from his pocket.

" This lighter, belonging to your husband, was found by the murdered woman's body . . . a woman savagely murdered by a lunatic."

He peered at Val and he was uneasily surprised to see that the impact of his words had no apparent effect on her.

" Obviously my husband lost the lighter and this killer found it."

" Charming to have such faith in an unstable mind," Hare said more roughly than he intended. " I think the police would have other ideas."

Val got to her feet.

" Then we will ask them. You are coming with me. We will see Captain Terrell and you will tell him what you are hinting at."

" Mrs. Burnett, we mustn't be impetuous," Hare said, not moving. He tossed the lighter into the air, caught it and then put it in his pocket. " Your husband wore a sports jacket when he left the hotel. When he was found, the jacket was missing. Happily for you both, I found it." With a quick movement, he got rid of the string around the brown paper parcel and produced the jacket. He spread it out on the sand. " These stains, madam, come from the ripped and murdered body of Sue Parnell !"

Val stood like a frozen statue, staring down at the coat she immediately recognised the coat Chris had been wearing on the terrace, a few minutes before he had disappeared. She looked at the ugly rust coloured blotches that covered the front of the coat. She felt her knees sag and very slowly, she collapsed onto the hot sand.

Hare watched her with the false sadness of a mortician.

" I'm very sorry, madam," he said gently. " Very very sorry. It would seem that your poor husband ran into this unfortunate

71

woman, and in a moment of complete madness, murdered her. This puts me in a very serious position . . . I . . ."

" Stop it, you vile old fake !" Val screamed at him. " I won't listen to you! Go away from me! Go away!"

Startled, Hare looked quickly over his shoulder and was relieved to see that there was no one close enough to have heard Val's outcry.

" Well, of course, if that is what you wish," he said with great diginity. " I never impose myself when I am not wanted. Then you want me to take this heavy responsibility and go to the police with this terrible and damning evidence?"

White faced, her eyes burning with fear and anger, Val stared at him.

" What else are you suggesting?"

" I have been struggling with my conscience," Hare said mildly. " Yours is a very well-known family. Your father is one of the most important men in the country. I felt I had to see you first before I went to the police. I thought you and also your father would not wish for your husband to be tried for the murder of a worthless prostitute, found guilty and put away for life behind the walls of a State Criminal Asylum. I felt the least I could do would be to talk to you and see if that is what you really wanted. It seemed to me that these two articles of deadly evidence could be destroyed and then no one but you and I would be any the wiser. That is why I have taken the trouble to come here this morning to consult with you, but if you would really prefer me to do my obvious duty, then regretfully, I will do so."

Val sat still, her hands in her lap, her face white. She remained like that for some moments, then she said quietly, without looking at Hare, " I understand . . . how much?"

Hare drew in a deep breath of air into his fat larded lungs. A nasty moment, he thought, but he had handled it well.

" A half a million dollars, madam," he said gently. " It is a reasonable sum. When you think what you are getting in return, it is a paltry sum." He took his card from his billfold and dropped it close to Val. " I will give the lighter and the jacket to the police at six o'clock this evening . . . at precisely six o'clock, unless, of course, you telephone me before then."

He rewrapped the packet, heaved himself to his feet. Then raising his hat to Val, he walked away across the sand, leaving big, widely spaced footprints behind him.

Chapter Six

TERRELL LOOKED up from a mass of reports he was reading as Beigler came into his office. As Beigler sat down and reached for the can of coffee that permanently stood on Terrell's desk, he said, "Nothing so far. We're still checking the list of her boy friends. We've reached number fifty-seven: so far they all have cast-iron alibis."

Terrell shrugged.

"They could all be in the clear, but we can't afford to miss out on one of them. It's my guess it is some sex nut who followed her and set on her. If I'm right, we'll have a job to find him. Nothing from the Service Stations?"

"No." Beigler sipped his coffee and lit a cigarette. "How about Hardy? Could be the Lang woman was lying when she gave him an alibi?"

"I thought of that, but why should Hardy want to kill her?" Terrell said, frowning. "So far he's operated without getting into trouble. Besides, I can't imagine he's the type to kill in that way."

"She could have had something on him, and he ripped her to make us think it was a sex killing."

"Yeah, that's right. I . . ."

The telephone bell rang. Terrell stopped short and lifted the receiver. He listened. Beigler saw his face tighten with surprise, then he said, "We'll be right with you. Don't touch a thing," and he hung up. He pushed back his chair and got to his feet. "Henekey's been found dead. Looks like someone's knocked him off. Come on . . . let's go."

Beigler crushed out his cigarette and moved fast from the office. As Terrell began the long walk down the corridor to the street, he could hear Beigler bawling for the Homicide Squad.

An hour and a half later, Dr. Lowis came from Henekey's cabin and crossed through a patch of sunlight to where Terrell and Beigler were waiting.

"He was murdered all right," Lowis said. "The killer worked him over before killing him. His body is a mass of cigarette burns. He was finally killed by someone putting a cushion over his face and sitting on it. He must have been a very heavy man. Henekey's nose is broken."

Terrell and Beigler exchanged glances. Then Terrell said, "Thanks, doc. Okay, if you're through, let's get him away."

When Henekey's body, watched by the tourists, had been taken away in the ambulance, Terrell and Beigler went into Henekey's cabin. The Homicide Squad had finished their work. Hess came over.

"No prints, Chief. There's one interesting thing . . ." He walked into the bathroom, followed by Terrell while Beigler remained in the doorway. Hess lifted a loose tile in the bathroom floor. "Could have been a hiding place for something. There's nothing in there now."

Terrell glanced into the cavity.

"Could be why he was worked over," he said. "Let's go look at the office safe."

It took an expert half an hour to get the safe open, but they found nothing to give them a lead on Henekey. They returned to the cabin. Hess and his men were leaving.

"Still nothing, Chief," Hess said. "This is a professional killing. Henekey went to bed around two o'clock. It's my bet the killer or killers were waiting for him in the cabin. The lock shows signs of being tampered with. They must have worn gloves. I can't turn up one fingerprint that isn't Henekey's."

Terrell grunted.

"Make a check of all the cabins. See if anyone heard

anything. Then check Henekey's prints. He may have a record."

Hess left, leaving the cabin door open. Terrell sat on the table while Beigler prowled around the cabin.

"What do you think, Chief?" Beigler asked finally. "Think this has any connection with the Parnell killing?"

Terrell took out his pipe and began to fill it.

"Yeah . . . seems more than possible. Could be Henekey was lying when he said he didn't know the girl. Could be he was holding back something and the Parnell killer came back, tortured him and finally killed him."

A shadow falling across the floor made both men look around sharply. Standing in the doorway was a little girl of around eight years of age. She was quite beautiful with blonde hair hanging below her shoulders. Her features were small and delicate, her eyes big and alert. She was wearing a blue and red check sunsuit and she was barefooted.

"Hello," she said. "Are you the police?"

Beigler was young enough to have no time for children. He scowled at her.

"Run away . . . get lost," he growled.

The girl looked inquiringly at Terrell.

"Who's the loud mouth with the ugly face?" she asked, resting her small, tanned body against the doorway.

"Hear me!" Beigler barked. "Run away!"

The child pursed her lips and blew him a raspberry that resounded through the still cabin.

"Drop dead!" she said with withering contempt. "If you're not all that tired of life, go suck your toenails!"

Terrell watched with amused interest. Beigler's face, dark red, was a study.

"If you were my daughter, I'd smack your bottom," he said furiously. "Run away!"

"If you were my father I'd have my mother's head examined," the child replied promptly.

Terrell turned a guffaw of laughter into a loud cough. Beigler glared at him, then with slow, deliberate steps, he began to advance on the child who faced him without fear and with such a sophisticated expression that Beigler came to a hesitant stand-still.

" If you touch me, I will charge you with rape," the child said.

Beigler took two hasty steps back and then looked helplessly at Terrell.

" What a little horror !" he exclaimed bitterly. " It's all very well for you to sit, grinning. I don't see anything funny in this little monster."

Terrell sat forward, resting his large hands on his knees.

" I'm the Chief of Police," he said and smiled at the child. " Who are you?"

The child drew a bare foot up her leg while she regarded Terrell with interest.

" My name's Angel Prescott. Who is the face over there?"

" He helps me," Terrell said gravely. " His name is Beigler."

" You really mean he helps you?" Angel looked astonished. " I wouldn't have believed it."

" He's very clever," Terrell said.

The child cocked her head on one side and studied Beigler who was slowly growing puce in the face.

" You never know, do you?" she said finally. " He looks like my uncle . . . he's poorly. They even have to feed him."

Beigler said with violence, " Get out of here ! Get lost !"

" He is noisy, isn't he?" Angel said. " I really came here because I wanted to help you."

" That's very nice of you, Angel," Terrell said. " I need all the help I can get. Come and sit down."

Beigler made a strangled noise and walked without thinking into the bathroom. Once inside he didn't know what to do with himself, so he came out again.

Angel, her blue eyes growing round, stared at him with morbid interest.

" Pheeew ! You were quick !" she exclaimed.

"Quick about what?" Beigler snarled, his face purple with rage.

"Don't expect me to discuss that sort of thing," Angel said primly. "I have been nicely brought up."

Beigler seemed to have trouble with his breathing. He looked around desperately as if in search of a weapon.

"I don't think I want to help you now," the child said to Terrell. "I see no reason why I should . . . Goodbye," and she walked with beautiful grace down the steps of the cabin and across to her own cabin.

"If she were my daughter, I'd take the skin off her bottom!" Beigler exploded. "Kids! Who wants kids these days! They . . ."

"Relax," Terrell said quietly. "She could have seen something. She lives right opposite. I'll go over and talk to her."

Beigler drew in a long deep breath.

"I'll see how Hess is making out," he said and walked stiffly away towards where the three police cars were parked.

Terrell grinned to himself, then knocking out his pipe, he walked over to the opposite cabin. He tapped on the door which was opened by a youngish, shabbily dressed woman with a harassed expression and who brushed back a lank strand of hair as she looked inquiringly at Terrell.

"Yes?"

"I'm Chief of Police Terrell," Terrell said. "I was talking to your daughter a moment ago. I would like to continue our conversation. Do you mind?"

"You've been talking to Angel?" The woman looked even more harassed. "But why?"

"She talked to me first, Terrell said. "I think she might be able to help me."

"Oh no! You don't know Angel! She is always romancing! It's about this murder, isn't it?"

"That's right."

"I'm sorry . . . I don't want Angel mixed up in that. She knows nothing. She's always romancing . . . really."

Angel joined her mother.

"Mummy, don't be a square," she said. "I know all about it. I saw them last night."

Mrs. Prescott looked helplessly at her daughter who regarded her with kindly contempt.

"Baby-girl, you know you didn't. You mustn't waste this gentleman's time. Now go in and do your painting."

Angel looked at Terrell.

"Mummy has always been stupid about me. She never believes anything I say. I saw them last night."

"Angel!" Mrs. Prescott exclaimed with feeble anger. "Do what I say! Go in and do your painting!"

The child lifted her beautiful little hands in a gesture of impatience.

"That's all she thinks about . . . she imagines I'm going to be a famous artist. I have less talent than a cow."

"She's really very talented," Mrs. Prescott said to Terrell. "You have no idea. She just says . . ."

"Would you let me talk to her?" Terrell asked gently. "May I come in?"

Mrs. Prescott again pushed her hair off her forehead. She looked distracted.

"Mummy! For goodness sake! Don't be so corny!" Angel said sharply. "You know you're dying for me to get some publicity." Giving her mother a little shove, she smiled at Terrell. "Come on in," and she turned and walked into the shabby sitting-room.

"Well, I suppose you'd better," Mrs. Prescott said helplessly. "She's really quite unusual for her age. I'm sure she can't tell you anything, but if you don't mind . . ."

"I don't mind," Terrell said and entered the room where Angel was already sitting, her hands clasped around her sun tanned knees.

"Mummy, would you go away," Angel said. "I can't talk to him with you fluttering around like a moth."

"You see?" Mrs. Prescott said with pride. "She isn't like an ordinary child. She . . ."

"Mummy! Please . . . !"

Mrs. Prescott hesitated, fluttered, then said as she was leaving the room, " She really doesn't know anything. She's always romancing."

There was a pause until the door shut, then Terrell took out his pipe and began to fill it.

" Tell me about it, Angel," he said. " What did you see last night?"

" Do you know what I want more than anything else in this world?" the child asked, staring intently at Terrell.

Terrell was startled.

" That's not answering my question. Listen, Angel, it is very important that I should find who killed Mr. Henekey. If you can help me, it's your duty to do so."

Angel scratched her left leg.

" I want a Teddy Bear as big as myself and that growls," she said. " That's what I want more than anything else in the world."

Terrell shifted. He paused to light his pipe.

" If you ask your mother nicely, she'll probably give it to you," he said. " Now who did you see last night?"

" Mummy never gives me anything. She hasn't any money. I'll never get a Teddy Bear as big as myself and that growls from her."

" Let's forget about the Teddy Bear," Terrell said firmly. " Who did you see last night? Was it someone going into Mr. Henekey's cabin?"

Angel scratched her right leg while she stared at Terrell, her blue eyes innocent and wide.

" Yes, that's right. There were two of them."

" Do you remember the time when you saw them?"

" It was five minutes to one. I have a clock by my bed. I woke up suddenly and the first thing I did was to put my torch on and look at my clock.

" Then what did you do?"

The child smiled at him.

" I don't remember."

" You looked out of the window," Terrel said patiently, " and you saw two men go into Mr. Henekey's cabin. That's right, isn't it?"

" I don't remember."

Terrell puffed at his pipe while he regarded the child, then he said, " Why did you say you could help me, Angel?"

" Oh, I can help you." She got to her feet and walked over to the radio. She switched it on. While waiting for the sound to come up, she said, " The thing I want more than anything else in the world is . . ."

" I know," Terrell said. " You've already told me, but I can't do anything about that. You must ask your mummy."

Dance music came over the air and Angel began to move her beautiful little body in time with the music.

" Goodbye," she said. " I'm busy now."

" Now listen, young lady," Terrell said sharply. " You have to tell me about these two men. Turn that off!"

Rather to his surprise she did so immediately and went back to her chair. She sat down and arranged her golden hair, lifting herself a little so she could see herself in the mirror on the opposite wall.

" What I want more than anything else in the world . . ." she began, stopped and smiled at Terrell who looked helplessly at her.

" Where do you sleep?" he asked.

" In the next room. Go and look."

He got up and left the room. Mrs. Prescott was standing nervously at the kitchen-doorway.

" May I go in?" Terrell said, pausing outside Angel's room.

She nodded and Terrell entered the tiny room. He crossed to the window and saw that he was looking straight at Henekey's cabin. The child's bed was close to the window. He saw that if she had sat up and looked out of the window she could have seen anyone entering Henekey's cabin.

Mrs. Prescott came to the door.

" Please don't take Angel seriously. She is too advanced for her age and she does romance. You really shouldn't listen to her."

"That's all right," Terrell said, "don't worry about it," and he went back into the sitting-room and shut the door.

Angel was standing before the mirror, examining herself with concentrated interest. She turned and smiled at him.

"If I bought you a Teddy Bear," Terrell said, "would you tell me who you saw going into Mr. Henekey's cabin?"

"Of course, but it has to be as big as myself and it has to growl."

"You really did see these two men? You see Angel, I would have to pay for your bear out of my own pocket. It wouldn't be very nice if you were telling stories just to get what you want."

The child shook her head.

"I wouldn't do that. There were two of them. I can describe them." She smiled brightly at him. "The trouble is I keep asking Mummy and she hasn't got any money. I do really want a Teddy Bear that's . . ."

"All right," Terrell, said, "I'll get it for you and then you'll help me . . . right?"

She gave him her charming smile.

"Thank you. Yes, I'll help you."

Terrell left the cabin and went in search of Beigler. When he had found him, he said, "Joe, I have an important job for you. I want you to drive fast to Miami and get a Teddy Bear, about three and a half feet tall that growls," Terrell said, keeping his face straight with an effort.

Beigler stared at Terrell.

"A Teddy Bear? Look, Chief . . ."

"It's an order, Joe. Get going. It's got to growl and make sure it is at least three and a half feet tall."

Beigler's face was a study. He drew in a long, choking breath and dragged at his shirt collar with hooked fingers.

"Who's going to pay for it?" he demanded.

Terrell handed over a fifty dollar bill.

"She's a cutie," he said and grinned. "She knows something, so we're doing a trade. Go get it, Joe, and hurry."

Beigler opened and shut his mouth, took the bill and then plodded away towards his car.

Val walked along the path of the ornamental garden to where her husband was sitting. She found him under a shady tree, listlessly staring down at his hands. Some twenty yards behind him, sat an Amazon of a nurse who gave Val an encouraging smile when she saw her, her knitting needles ceaselessly clicking.

There was a vacant chair near Chris's, and as Val drew nearer, he looked up, frowned, then smiled and reaching out, pulled the chair closer to him.

" Hello," he said. " I was wondering if you were coming."

" I've been waiting all the morning to come," she said. " How are you darling?"

" I'm all right. What have you been doing with yourself?" He looked steadily at her. The blankness of his eyes tugged at her heart. " You're looking very brown. Been swimming?"

" Yes. The water is marvellous." She groped for something else to say but could find nothing. The weight of what Homer Hare had said paralysed her mind.

" Have you thought more about the divorce?" Chris asked abruptly. " Did you talk to your father?"

" I don't want a divorce, darling."

His mouth twitched, and he suddenly looked irritable.

" You haven't been thinking about it. You mustn't spend all your time enjoying yourself . . . you must think sometimes."

She recalled the long hours before lunch when she had sat on the beach after Hare had plodded away and what her thoughts had been.

" I just don't want to lose you, Chris."

" She's watching us, isn't she?" he said. " She's quite clever. She keeps out of sight, but I know she's there. You must get a divorce, Val. I'll never get any better."

" Oh, you will," Val said earnestly. " I know how you must feel. This is something that has happened . . . it could have happened to me. I would be so happy to know that if it had

83

happened to me you would still want me as I want you."

He didn't seem to be listening. He stared across the close cut lawn, his face expressionless.

" Well, all right, if you don't want a divorce, then you have only yourself to blame," he said.

" Yes, I know, Chris."

There was a long, long silence, then Val said, " Have you thought about that night you went away . . . when you couldn't remember anything?"

He leaned back in his chair. She wasn't sure if he had heard what she had said.

" She's still there, isn't she? I won't give her the satisfaction of looking at her, but she is still there?"

" Yes." Val longed for a cigarette, but knowing Chris now no longer smoked, she resisted the urge. " That night, Chris . . ."

" Why do you ask?" He stared curiously at her.

" I just wondered if you remember now what happened."

He hesitated, frowning and not looking at her.

" I suppose I do. It's all rather confused." He glanced slyly over his shoulder at the nurse, then as the nurse paused in her knitting to look at him, he quickly turned away. " She's always watching me," he went on, " like that other woman. She knew I wasn't normal."

" What other woman, Chris?"

" The one I met. I was sitting waiting for someone to give me a lift back to the hotel. I had smashed up the car. I think I must have gone to sleep or something. I came to when the car hit the tree." He rubbed the back of his hand across his eyes, frowning. " You don't want to be bothered with all this. Have you heard from your father? Is he back in New York?"

" Yes, he's back," Val said quietly. " What happened when the car hit the tree?"

" After waiting a bit I started to walk. I walked some way. I tried to get cars to stop, but none of them would. I got bored and when I saw a car coming, I stepped in front of it. It was dark by then. I really hoped it would knock me down. I was so bored with myself, but it didn't. There was this woman . . ."

Val waited, but he seemed to have forgotten what he was saying and just sat there limply staring into space.

"Tell me about her," Val said at last.

"About who?"

"This woman who stopped."

"There's nothing to tell. She stopped . . . that's all."

Val had a sudden idea he was concealing something from her that frightened him. She regarded him, feeling a cold sensation building up around her heart.

"Did she talk to you?"

He moved restlessly.

"We drove some way. Yes, she talked. I can't remember what about . . . I think I was sorry for her somehow."

"What was she like?"

"I don't know." He frowned. "It's odd, but when I think of her, I think of elephants."

Val was startled.

"But, why? Was she so big then?"

"No . . . I don't think so. I honestly don't remember anything about her except the elephants." He looked over his shoulder at the nurse. "She thinks I could become violent. Did you know?"

"Why should you become violent?" Val asked, her mouth suddenly turning dry.

"People in my state often do."

Val couldn't bear to listen to this kind of talk.

"Chris, I need some money. I haven't enough in my account. Would you sign a blank cheque for me? I've brought your cheque book along."

He sat motionless for so long she wasn't sure if he had heard what she had said, then slowly, he turned his head and the suspicious expression in his eyes sent a chill up her spine.

"How much do you want?"

"Oh, a few thousand dollars." Val tried unsuccessfully to sound casual. "You see, Chris, we have a lot of expenses. I've decided not to let daddy pay the hotel bill and . . ."

"You don't have to lie about it," he said. "Exactly how much money do you want?"

Val sat motionless. She would have to ask her father, she told herself hopelessly. She could lie to him, but she had never succeeded in lying to Chris.

"I can manage, Chris. Let's forget it."

He sat forward so abruptly, the nurse watching paused in her knitting, ready to rise to her feet.

"Is someone blackmailing you about me?" he asked, staring at Val. "Is that it?"

She hesitated, then realising, he must be told, said "Yes, Chris."

He slumped down in the chair.

"How much does he want?"

"Twenty thousand dollars."

"It's not much, is it? Well, we must tell the police. One should never pay blackmail. I'll admit I did it, and that will be that. If we pay this man, he will go on making demands . . . blackmailers always do."

"Admit you did *what*?" Val exclaimed, stiffening.

"Whatever the man says I did. I told you, didn't I, that I could have done anything . . . even murdered someone." He looked away from her, his long, slim fingers moving restlessly up and down his thighs. "Last night I dreamed I killed a woman. I expect that's what I have done . . . killed some woman. Is that what he says I did?"

"Stop it!" Val said fiercely. "You don't know what you are saying! You haven't killed anyone!"

"Is that what he says I did?" he repeated looking up at her. Then as she said nothing, he suddenly shrugged. "What's money, anyway? Give me the cheque book."

She took the cheque book from her bag and gave it to him with a pen. He signed three blank cheques and then handed her back the cheque book.

"I'll never come out of here, so you may as well have the use of my money. I leave it to you, Val. Clear the account and put the money in your account."

Val put the cheque book back in her bag. Her hands were shaking and she was very white.

" Who was the woman I killed, Val?" he asked.

" There was no woman. You didn't do anything! I know you didn't!"

" I suppose it is better to pay blackmail. On second thoughts, your father would hate me to be tried for murder, wouldn't he?"

" You wouldn't be tried for murder, darling. You haven't done anything."

" Who is this man who is blackmailing us?"

" Oh, just a man. Don't worry about him."

" If he hadn't convinced you, you wouldn't be paying him, would you?"

" Don't let's talk any more about it. I'm going, but I'll see you tomorrow."

" You don't really have to bother. I manage sitting here on my own," he said indifferently and closed his eyes.

In despair, she turned and walked away.

Chapter Seven

SAM KARSH was waiting when Homer Hare came heavily into his office after a long and excellent lunch.

"Well, I thought you were in jug by now," Karsh said. "What happened?"

"Sammy, you must learn to trust me. We're onto a very good thing . . . like I told you. The little lady has everything to gain and a husband to lose."

"Yeah . . . from what I hear, she's lost him already."

Hare dismissed this with a wave of his hand.

"She's in love with him," he said. "Knowing human nature the way I do, when a woman is stupid enough to fall in love, she is a sucker for me." He looked at the strap watch on his fat wrist. "I think I can call her now. She'll have had time to make up her mind.

"This idea of yours doesn't jell with me," Karsh said uneasily. "We've never stuck our necks out this far. Are you sure she won't bleat to the cops?"

"She won't. We've never stuck our necks out this far because we have never had the chance of picking up half a million bucks," Hare said. Lifting the telephone receiver, he asked Lucille to connect him with the Spanish Bay hotel.

Val had just got back from her visit to the sanatorium and was about to sit down before the open window when the telephone bell buzzed. She hesitated, then crossing the room, she answered the call.

"Is that Mrs. Burnett?"

She immediately recognised the dreaded wheezy voice. She

controlled the impulse to slam down the receiver. She said,
" Yes."

" We talked this morning." She could hear the fat man
struggling with his breath. " Is it yes or no, madam?"

" It's yes, but I need time," Val said, aware her voice was
unsteady. " I can pay twenty thousand tomorrow. I need two
weeks before I pay the rest."

" That would be satisfactory. In cash, if you please. Would
you be good enough to come to my office tomorrow at eleven
and bring the cash? You have my address. We will then be
able to discuss how the rest of the money is to be paid."

" I'll do that," Val said and hung up. She stared across the
room for some moments, then she abruptly called the Florida
Banking Corporation and asked to speak to the manager. She
had only to mention her name to be put through immediately.

Henry Thresby, the manager of the bank, was warned by his
secretary that the daughter of Charles Travers was on the line.

" Good afternoon, Mrs. Burnett," he said in his bright, alert
business voice. " Is there something I may do for you?"

" Yes, please," Val told him. " I want twenty thousand dollars.
I will be in tomorrow morning. I'll bring my husband's
cheque.

" Certainly. I'll have the money ready for you. There'll be no
difficulty about that."

" I want the money in one hundred dollar bills," Val went
on, hesitated, then said, " I would be glad if you would take a
note of the numbers of all the bills and let me have the numbers.
Would you also please arrange to have the money done up in a
parcel and sealed with the bank's seal?

Thresby's long experience in banking affairs allowed his tone
to remain normal while his expression became startled.

" Certainly . . . only too happy, Mrs. Burnett. The parcel will
be ready for you when you come. Do you wish to check the
amount before the parcel is sealed?"

" That won't be necessary. I'll be at the bank about ten
o'clock."

"Everything will be ready and arranged as you wish, Mrs. Burnett."

"Thank you," and Val hung up.

Thresby, a small dapper man with a balding head and shrewd eyes, pushed back his chair. He stared into space, frowning. He was a conscientious banker. He had been pleased to have obtained Chris Burnett's account when the Burnetts had come to stay at the Spanish Bay hotel. He was aware of the importance of these two young people . . . even more aware of their connection with the great Charles Travers. These instructions, given him by Mrs. Burnett, set an alarm ringing in his mind. Twenty thousand dollars, the numbers to be recorded and the money to be put in a sealed parcel meant to him either ransom or blackmail money.

He lit a cigarette and pondered the problem. He and Chief of Police Terrell had gone to school together. They spent holidays, fishing together. He knew he could rely on Terrell's discretion. Although he felt uneasy that he was going beyond the strict letter of his duty, he didn't hesitate for long. He reached for the telephone and asked to be connected with Police Headquarters. Sergeant Thames, the desk sergeant, told him that Terrell was out. He had no idea when he would be back.

"This is important, Sergeant. Will you ask the Chief to call me at my home any time after six o'clock?"

Sergeant Thames said he would do that.

Joe Beigler walked from the toy store carrying under his arm a large brown paper parcel containing an enormous Teddy Bear. He felt a vindictive pleasure that the Bear had cost seventy-five dollars. If the Chief was dumb enough to pander to this little horror, he thought, then it was his bad luck if he was to be seventy-five dollars out of pocket.

He arrived back at the motel to find Terrell waiting for him. He was pleased to see his Chief's face fall when he told him he owed him another twenty-five dollars.

"I'll give it to you tomorrow," Terrell said and taking the parcel he walked over to the Prescott's cabin.

Beigler went to the cafeteria and devoured a couple of hamburgers, washed down with ice-cold beer. As he was about to order a second beer, he saw Terrell come out of the Prescott's cabin and look around for him. He paid his check and went out to Terrell.

"It's paid off," Terrell said. "I guess I know who these two guys are, but I want you to hear what she's told me and see if you agree with me."

Beigler followed him into the cabin where Angel was sitting, looking at the Teddy Bear with wonder and love while Mrs. Prescott, red with embarrassment, stood by the window, watching her daughter.

"Angel, let's go over it all again," Terrell said. "Just once more."

She smiled at him.

"Yes." She looked at Beigler. "Thank you for getting me my Teddy. You're cleverer than you look."

Beigler scowled at her, sat down at the table and opened his notebook.

"Go ahead, Angel," Terrell said, sitting down. "You woke up at five minutes to one. You put on your torch and looked at your clock. That's right, isn't it?"

"Yes," the child said. "I looked out of the window and I saw . . ."

"Why did you look out of the window?" Terrell interrupted.

"I wanted to see if there was a moon. I like looking at the moon."

"And was there a moon?"

"It was dark, but I could see the moon behind a cloud. Then I saw two men walking down the lane between the cabins. They had to pass under those lights in the tree at the far end of the lane. I saw them clearly."

"You saw them well enough to recognise them again?"

"I would recognise the fat man, but I don't think I would recognise the nigger. He . . ."

"Angel! You mustn't say nigger," Mrs. Prescott broke in. "You should say he was a coloured man."

91

Angel gave her mother an irritable look and then went on, "All niggers look alike to me, but the other man I'd know anywhere."

"Before you describe him, tell me what these two did."

"Well, they walked to Mr. Henekey's cabin and went up onto the porch. My window was open and I heard them whispering. I couldn't hear what they were saying. It was too dark there to see what they were doing, but I heard the door creak open and they went inside."

"Then what did you do."

"I waited because I wondered what they were doing in Mr. Henekey's cabin. I got sleepy, and when Mr. Henekey arrived. I thought he would find out for himself, so I went to sleep."

"You are sure they didn't leave before Henekey arrived?"

"No, they were in the cabin all the time. They didn't leave."

"All right, Angel, now tell me about the fat man."

"He was very big and very fat. He was the biggest and fattest man I have ever seen."

"You told me he was about Sergeant Beigler's age," Terrell said, "and he wore a blue shirt and dark trousers. That's right, isn't it?"

"Yes."

"And you're sure his companion was coloured?"

"Oh yes. He had on a yellow and white sweat shirt, and blue jeans."

"And there was something else that struck you about the fat man?" Terrell said. "Wasn't there?"

Angel hid her face in the fur of the bear. She giggled.

"Oh, yes. He was a pansy. I know all about *them* because my friend, Doris, told me. She knows all about *them* because her brother is one of them. I could tell that was what he was by his walk."

"Angel!" Mrs. Prescott exclaimed, horrified. "You really . . ."

"Please!" Terrell said sharply. "This is important," to Angel: "Just how did he walk?"

92

The child got to her feet and began to mince around the room. Her imitation of the walk of a homosexual was so convincing that even Beigler had to grin.

She stopped and looked at Terrell.

" Like that."

" I want you to wait here for a little while," Terrell said. " Then I hope you will help me some more."

" Now I have my bear, I'll help you as much as I can," Angel said gravely. She went over to the bear and hugged it, looking at Terrell, her eyes adoring.

Pleased, Terrell smiled and got up. He nodded to Beigler and the two men went out into the sunshine.

" Well, you name them, Joe," Terrell said.

" Jacko Smith and Moe Lincoln," Beigler said without hesitation. " Can't be anyone else."

" Hardy's body guard. Looks as if some of the pieces are falling into place. But we have to be sure. The next move is to show Jacko to the child and see if she can recognise him."

" What do we do?" Beigler rubbed his jaw. " Bring him in . . . have a line-up and let the kid finger him?"

Terrell shook his head. He looked at his watch. The time was twenty minutes past five.

" We'll drive her to the Coral bar. Jacko usually shows there around half-past six. We'll park within sight, and she can spot him when he goes into the bar. If she recognises him, we'll bring him in and have a line-up."

They went back to the cabin.

" I want your daughter to come along with us," Terrell said to Mrs. Prescott. " It is essential that she identifies this man. You'll come too, of course."

" Oh, no, she won't," Angel said firmly. " If she comes, then I won't help you. Just me and Teddy."

" Now, Baby-girl," Mrs. Prescott said helplessly, " you mustn't be naughty. You can't go alone with these gentlemen."

" Then I'm not going at all," Angel said in a decided voice and putting her arms around her bear, she dragged it off the settee and began to move to the door.

" She'll be all right with me." Terrell said. " I'll bring her right back, Mrs. Prescott. This is important police business."

Mrs. Prescott started to say something when Angel said, " I'll see you later, Mummy," and walked briskly from the cabin to where the police cars were parked.

" If she was my daughter, I'd . . ." Beigler began, his face red with indignation.

Mrs. Prescott drew herself up.

" I'm glad she isn't!" she said. " I don't care for anyone criticising my child and I'll thank you not to pass such remarks!"

Beigler looked helplessly at Terrell, closed his notebook and followed his Chief out and across to where Angel waited for them impatiently.

Moe Lincoln lay back in the barber's chair, feeling the keen edge of the razor pass over his black cheek. His eyes were closed, his vicious face in repose as he relaxed to the soft hands of Toey Marsh who had been trying for months to persuade Moe to leave Jacko and come to live with him.

Toey was half Chinese, half Pole : a fat little man, nudging fifty with henna dyed hair, almond shaped eyes and a round fat face. He was considered one of the best barbers in the district and Moe always had an evening shave from him before going out to set the town alight with Jacko.

" What's the time, baby?" Moe asked, keeping his eyes shut.

" Nearly half-past six," Toey told him after consulting his watch. " What are you doing tonight? Would you like to come back to my place. I'm throwing a party. Chinese food, and there's a boy . . ."

" I've got a date with Jacko," Moe said who liked to torture Toey. " Why should I want to go to your crummy joint?"

Toey sighed. He applied a hot towel to Moe's face and leaving him for a moment, he wandered to the shop window to look out onto the street.

" That's funny," he said. " What are *they* doing, I wonder?"

"Who, dopey?" Moe asked, pressing the hot towel to his face and breathing in the menthol fumes coming from the towel.

"The cops . . . out there in a car with a little girl," Toey said, coming over to change the towel.

Moe stiffened. He snatched off the towel, slid out of the chair and went to the window. He stared at the police car. It was in a parking bay fifty yards or so from the entrance to the Coral bar.

"What's the matter?" Toey asked.

"Shut your flap!" Moe snarled. "Gimme a towel." Without taking his eyes off the police car, he reached out his lean black hand and snatched the towel Toey gave him. He hurriedly wiped his face and the back of his neck and then threw the towel from him.

He watched : then he saw Jacko Smith come waddling down the street.

Jacko always parked his pink and blue Cadillac at the far end of the street. He believed the short walk from the parking lot to the Coral bar helped to keep down his weight. He came along, a handkerchief in his fat hand, wearing the light blue shirt, and black baggy trousers he had worn the previous night. From time to time, he dabbed at his white unhealthy looking face with the handkerchief.

Terrell said sharply, "Angel, look down the road."

Angel, who had been playing with her bear, looked up and saw Jacko as he came towards them.

"That's him!" she whispered excitedly and pointed her small finger towards Jacko who had paused for a brief moment outside the Coral bar.

"Are you sure?" Terrell asked.

"Yes! That's him!"

Moe, watching, saw her point at Jacko and his black face creased into a vicious snarl. He realised at once that this child was identifying Jacko to the cops and this could only mean one thing! This child had seen them enter Henekey's cabin!

Toey, standing behind him, and watching what was going on, said, "What is it, honey? She fingering Jacko?"

Moe turned savagely on him.

"Shut it! Wipe it out of your mind! You want to stay alive, Toey?"

At the sight of the murderous gleam in the vicious black eyes, Toey quailed.

"I never saw a thing!" he stammered. "Honest, I never . . ."

"Shut it!" Moe snarled.

He watched Beigler start the car engine and then drive away towards headquarters.

Moe paused only long enough to glare at Toey.

"Remember . . . if you've seen anything, Toey, I'll slit you," he said, and then moving fast he ran across the street into the Coral bar.

Jacko was about to order a shot of whisky and a beer chaser when Moe came in.

Moe said, "Let's get out of here, Jacko, and fast!"

The expression in Moe's gleaming eyes was enough for Jacko. He waddled after Moe, moving his enormous legs as fast as he could and panting.

The barman watched them go, grimaced, and then returned to his task of washing glasses.

It wasn't until eight-ten o'clock that Terrell drove into his garage. He was feeling hot and tired. Having driven Angel Prescott back to the Park Motel, he was now looking forward to a shower and a good dinner.

His wife opened the front door as he came up the drive. They kissed, then Terrell asked the age old question husbands always ask, "What's for dinner?"

"Chicken," Caroline said. "It'll be ready in half-an-hour, but you'll have to call Henry first.

Terrel walked into the lounge and began to shed his jacket and tie.

"Henry?" He looked at Caroline in surprise. "What's he want?"

"He said it was important. You call him while I get you a drink."

96

Terrell hesitated, then seeing the stern expression in his wife's eyes, he grinned and went over to the telephone. He dialled Henry Thresby's home number, and while he waited for the connection, he reached out a grateful hand for the whisky and soda, clinking with ice, that Caroline offered him.

Thresby came on the line.

"Frank? I'm sorry to disturb you, but I have something that's bothering me. I thought I would get your advice and hear what you have to say."

At the sound of Thresby's anxious tone, Terrell became alert.

"Go ahead, Henry. What is it?"

Briefly, Thresby told him about the telephone call he had had from Val Burnett.

"I could be sticking my neck out, but to me, it sounds as if Mrs. Burnett could be in trouble," Thresby concluded. "Now look, Frank, we have to be mighty careful about this. If it means nothing, Travers could descend on me, and I could lose my job."

"I think you have every reason to be worried," Terrell said. "I'm glad you called me. Now look, Henry, you leave this to me. Just forget it, will you? The less you know about it, the better. I'll take care of it."

"For goodness sake, be careful!"

"You know me," Terrell said quietly. "I'll handle it. Did you keep a copy of the numbers of the bills?"

"Yes, of course."

"Let me have the list. Send it here. That way it won't get into the wrong hands. Okay, Henry, relax. I'll fix it," and he hung up.

Seeing the furrow between his brows, Caroline knew better than to ask questions. She went into the kitchen to serve up the meal.

Terrell called headquarters. When Beigler came on the line, Terrell asked, "Got Jacko Smith yet?"

"Not yet. I have men shaking down the clubs. They should pick him up any time now."

"Have you someone staked out outside Smith's apartment?"

97

Terrell knew he was wasting his breath as Beigler was as efficient as himself, but he had to ask.

" Walker and Lucas are covering the joint."

" I want that fat slob fast."

" We'll have him before midnight. He's playing cards in some hole. It's just a matter of finding where he's playing."

" Joe . . . there's something else," Terrell said. " Tell Jacobs to come out here. He's on duty, isn't he?"

" Why, sure."

" Tell him to hustle over. If he comes fast enough, he can have a chicken dinner with me."

Beigler snorted.

" If there's one way to get Max to move fast, it's the offer of a free meal."

As Terrell was sitting down at the table, reaching for the carving knife and fork, the front door bell rang. He grinned at his wife.

" That's Max. Put a plate for him. He must have bust every speed record in the State."

Max Jacobs, a lean, tall, first-year cop, came into the lounge and looked with round eyes at the perfectly cooked chicken. Terrell pointed with the carving knife to a chair.

" We'll eat first," he said, " then talk. I have a job for you."

Later, when Caroline was washing up, Terrell, his pipe drawing well, told Jacobs about Val Burnett.

" Looks like a blackmail set up," he concluded. " We can't move in unless she calls us, but we can be ready. I want you to be outside the bank at nine o'clock tomorrow morning. When Mrs. Burnett leaves, make sure she has the money with her and then follow her. Now look, Max it is vitally important she gets no idea you are following her, so watch your step. Find out where she takes the money. If she goes back to her hotel, see Dulac and tell him you're from me. Ask him to let you know if anyone goes up to her suite. If anyone does, follow whoever it is. Don't consult the hotel detective. I don't trust him. Got all that?"

Jacobs nodded.

"Okay, Chief, I'll handle it," and he got to his feet. "I'll be on the job at nine tomorrow."

When he had gone, Terrell called police headquarters. He asked Beigler if there was any news yet of Jacko Smith.

"Nothing so far, Chief," Beigler said. "I'm getting reports continually, but he isn't in his usual haunts."

"Send out a State alarm," Terrell said. "I want him fast. Turn the heat on, Joe. I'm coming down."

"Okay," Beigler said, "but you don't have to come down. I can handle it."

"I know you can," Terrell said, "but I'm coming."

Spike Calder was a tall, emaciated Negro with flat snake's eyes and a perpetual grin that revealed big, gleaming white teeth. He ran the Bo-Bo Club on the waterfront that was frequented by queers and gamblers from the dock quarter of Miami.

The big advantage of the club was that it had a secret room for meetings below the main bar and restaurant, so cunningly hidden that the police hadn't so far discovered it.

It was in this room that Jacko Smith and Moe Lincoln were now sitting, whisky and beer chasers on the table before them.

Moe had told Jacko what he had seen and Jacko was now considering what to do.

"We mustn't take any risks," he said finally. "We've got to find out if this kid did see anything. Looks like she's at the motel, but we got to find out for sure."

Moe nodded. This made sense to him.

"You stick right here, baby," he said. "I'll get Hoppy to go out to the motel and sniff around."

"Watch yourself," Jacko said, patting Moe's arm.

"Don't worry about me, baby," and Moe went up the stairs, peered through the peep-hole to make sure there was no one around then let himself out of the secret room.

Hoppy Lincoln, Moe's younger brother was losing money in a crap game when Moe finally found him. Seeing his brother, he left the game and joined him.

Moe told him what he wanted him to do.

"Take my car," Moe said, "and snap it up. I want you back here pronto."

Hoppy began to whine, but at the sight of the two five dollar bills Joe thrust at him, he suddenly grinned.

"Okay, sweetie," he said. I'm on my way."

The two brothers left the gambling room and Hoppy went quickly across the street to where Moe had parked his car. He got in and drove away.

Moe moved through the back alleys, avoiding the main streets until he was within sight of the Bo-Bo Club. He paused in the shadows.

Walking towards the club were two police officers. Moe recognised them immediately. He remained motionless like a black shadow and saw them enter the club.

The police officers, Marshall and Lepski, pushed their way through to the crowded bar where Spike Calder was mixing drinks.

At the sight of them, the men and women in the room suddenly became silent. Three or four of them edged towards the exit. The rest stared sullenly at the two officers, their eyes glittering, their hatred showing in their tense faces.

Spike put down the cocktail mixer and eyed the two men cautiously. So far he had never been in trouble with the police, and if he could avoid it, he was determined to steer clear of police trouble.

"Evenin', gents," he said with an expansive smile. "What'll you have?"

"Seen Jacko Smith?" Marshall asked. He was a short, heavily built man with muscles of a boxer and a hard, battered face.

"Not yet," Spike lied. "Maybe he'll be in in a little while, but he hasn't shown yet."

Lepski, thin, wiry and tough, leaned against the bar counter.

"Listen, Smokey, think twice before you open that drain in your face," he said softly. "We're looking for Jacko . . . could be a murder charge. If you know where he is, now's the time to flex your tonsils and sing. If we find he's here or he's been here, you're going inside. I'd like to work you over. The best sound in this stinking town to me is the moans of a black boy."

Spike's smile slipped a little.

" I'd tell you if he was here. Look around, mister and see for yourself. I haven't seen him since yesterday night."

The two police officers looked around the big room and then at each other.

" If he comes in, call headquarters. That way you'll keep out of trouble."

Lepski stared at Spike for a long cruel moment, then jerking his head at Marshall, he left the bar.

Moe, hidden in the shadows, watched the two police officers walk down the street and enter yet another gambling cellar.

Like a black ghost, he slid across the street and down the back entrance to the Bo-Bo Club. He paused long enough to listen and make sure there was no one about, then he fumbled for the hidden catch that opened the door into the secret room, slipped into the darkness, shut the door, then switched on the light. As he came down the stairs leading into the room where Jacko Smith was lolling, Spike Calder came in from the other hidden entrance.

Moe looked at Spike, his eyes alert. Spike ignored Moe and walked over to Jacko.

" On your way," Spike said softly. " Up with the fat and dust."

Jacko stared at him.

" You don't talk that way to me, black boy," he said furiously. " When I want to go, I'll go, but not before."

" You'll heave the guts out right now," Spike said. " The cops have been here. They're looking for you. I don't cover anyone as hot as you, Jacko. On your way."

Moe said, " He stays right here." He had his broad bladed knife in his hand. " You want me to carve you a little, nigger?"

Spike smiled.

" You'll have to grow a lot bigger and a lot tougher to carve me," he said. " Try it and see," and a long stabbing knife jumped into his hand.

Moe snarled at him and began to move forward.

"Stop it!" Jacko said sharply.

Moe slid the knife back into its sheath. He moved further away from Spike to give himself the chance to get the knife out again should Spike show signs of attacking him.

"What's biting you, Spike?" Jacko asked with deceptive mildness. "What did the cops say?"

"Plenty," Spike said. "They are looking for you. They're talking about a murder charge. That's too hot for me. On your way, Jacko, and keep clear of me."

Jacko and Moe exchanged glances. Jacko began to sweat. There was a long pause, then Moe said, "Okay, Spike, we'll go, but they're nuts. Jacko hasn't killed anyone."

Jacko heaved himself to his feet. Spike was watching Moe which was stupid as Jacko was much closer to him. With a movement, terrifyingly swift for a man of his size, Jacko grabbed the whisky bottle and slammed it across Spike's face with bone crushing violence. Spike reeled back, dropping his knife. Moe sprang like a black cat at him as he collapsed on the floor. His black hand, holding the gleaming knife, flashed up and down twice, then he got to his feet. He bent over Spike's lifeless body and wiped the blade of the knife clean on Spike's shirt, then he looked at Jacko.

"He was chickening out," he said. "Better this way. What do we do now?"

Jacko lowered his great body onto the chair. He took out a carton of chocolates and began to stuff chocolates into his mouth.

"We're getting into the real crap now, boysie," he said, his mouth full. "We'd better get out . . . but where do we go?"

"It must be Henekey," Moe said, sitting on the table, swinging his legs. "The kid must have seen us. We've got to fix her, baby. Without her, without Spike, we should be in the clear. I'll go down to the motel and knock her off."

Jacko nodded.

"But where do I go?"

Moe frowned as he swung his legs, then he suddenly grinned.

"Go to Hardy. He got us into this mess. Go to him, baby. He'll have to cover you for the night. By tomorrow you'll be in the clear. Without the kid, they haven't a thing on us."

"Is there anyone else?" Jacko asked. "Anyone who could fix us?"

Moe thought of Toey. Toey had seen the kid finger Jacko. He hesitated. It was a pity to get rid of Toey as he was a good barber, but Moe didn't hesitate for long.

He told Jacko about Toey.

Jacko looked sad. Toey also cut Jacko's hair, but he realised that once Toey knew the cops were looking for him on a murder charge, he would turn soft.

"Fix him too," he said and got to his feet. "You take me to Hardy in my car, and then fix Toey. Then you go to the motel and fix the kid."

"Yes, sweetie," Moe said. "You leave it all to me."

The two of them, one gross, the other hard and slim, moved silently out of the secret room and into the darkness of the night.

Chapter Eight

GINA LANG sat on the bed, occupied in painting her toenails while she listened to a Sinatra L.P. playing in the lounge.

The time was a little after ten-thirty. Lee Hardy had said he would be back by eleven, and then they would go to the Coral Club for a drink before taking in a midnight movie.

Her task completed, Gina stood up. She was wearing a bra and black lace pants. She surveyed herself in the full length mirror with shrewd, searching eyes. She was twenty-three. She had had her first affair at the age of fourteen with a man she had long forgotten. Since then, she had spent the past nine years drifting from one man's bed to another's. During this sexual pilgrimage she had acquired two mink coats, a diamond necklace, various other pieces of jewellery of lesser value and fifteen thousand dollars in the bank. Looking at herself now in the mirror, she searched for any sign of her past life, and was pleased to see that nothing so far had left a scar on her attractiveness. Her body was firm and beautifully made. Her face amused her, and she knew fascinated men, but she wasn't too sure about her eyes. She tried to soften their expression, but failed. Well, she thought, shrugging at least they'll warn Lee not to fool around with any other woman now, and he needs the warning!

She had been living with Lee Hardy now for three months. Their meeting had been casual. When she discovered he had money, a Cadillac and a penthouse, she was happy to leave the party with him at which they had met. They went back to his luxury home.

Then something happened that she least expected. She

104

found he was not only an extremely accomplished lover, but his handsomeness and his gaiety turned the routine romp in bed into a fierce possessive love. This had never happened to her before, and it threw her off balance. She suggested she should move into the pent house, and after only a moment's hesitation, Hardy had agreed. He was getting bored with continually chasing women, breaking down their resistance, buying them presents, quarrelling with them, and finally trying to get rid of them. He found Gina intriguing, sexually exciting and a good cook.

This state of affairs lasted some two months, then Hardy, from force of habit, began to look around for fresh diversions, but he quickly discovered this could be dangerous. He was shocked by Gina's vicious temper. The row they had had when he had smiled at a girl in a nightclub was heard by everyone in the block. There was nothing he could do with her. She was like a demented wild cat. It was only when he rashly promised never to look at another woman again that she calmed down. Later, he tried to prepare himself to tell her to get out of his pent house, but he hesitated, knowing he would never find a girl as intriguing as she was, and also the memory of her fury still scared him.

Satisfied that she now had hooked him, Gina was considering the best way to get him to marry her. She was sick of forever hunting for a new and substantial meal ticket, and having satisfied herself that Hardy was smart enough to keep with the big money, there seemed no reason why they shouldn't get married. So this evening, she planned to force his hand.

For the next twenty minutes, she made herself as attractive as she could, and the result was impressive for Gina was an artist in making the best of herself. As she was struggling to pull the zipper up on the gold lamé dress that fitted her like a second skin, she heard the front door bell ring.

She looked at the clock on her bedside table. It was nearly eleven. She thought: Lee's forgotten his key again! Well, at least, for a change, he's punctual.

She ran to the front door and opened it. It came as a considerable shock when she saw Jacko Smith standing in the corridor, his great fat face dripping with sweat and the smell of sweat oozing from him.

She knew Jacko Smith was Hardy's strong-arm man. She had seen him from time to time on the race tracks, but she had never spoken to him. She had loathed the sight of him as soon as she had seen him. The fact he was a homosexual turned her loathing into revulsion. If there was a breed of perverts Gina hated most it was the homosexual.

"Where is Hardy?" Jacko demanded, eyeing Gina with as much contempt as she was eyeing him. He regarded all women as unworthy of his consideration.

"He's out!" Gina snapped and began to close the door. To her dismay, Jacko moved forward with the power and force of an Army tank. He rode her back into the lobby and shut the front door.

"Get out of here!" Gina cried shrilly. "How dare you force your way in here!"

"Shut up!" Jacko snarled. "This is business!"

"If you think you can push your filthy way . . ."

"Shut up!" Jacko repeated. "Hardy is in trouble. I'm in trouble. Where is he?"

Gina looked closely at the fat man. The restless movement of his little eyes, the sweat that soaked his shirt and the way his mouth tightened and loosened began to frighten her.

"What's happened?" she demanded.

He waddled past her into the lounge and seeing the cocktail cabinet, he crossed to it and poured himself three fingers of Scotch, added a little charge water and greedily gulped down the drink.

She stood in the doorway, glaring at him.

"What is it? The police?"

"Yes," Jacko said and poured himself another drink. "Where is he?"

"He said he would be back by eleven. It's eleven now. What's happened?"

"He'll tell you if he wants you to know," Jacko said. "I'll wait."

"Not here . . . you won't. Get out!"

Jacko looked at her, his little eyes gleaming viciously.

"Screw you," he said. "You want me to push that flat nose of yours through the back of your head?"

Gina turned abruptly and went into her bedroom, shutting and locking the door.

Trouble! Police! She clenched her fists, her eyes glittering. What had Lee done?

She sat on the bed and waited for his return.

Toey Marsh was enjoying himself. He liked nothing better than to throw a party with Chinese food prepared by himself for a few boy friends, and after the eating, to put on discs on the gramophone and have a social evening lasting to three o'clock in the morning. His party was obviously a big success. He stood by the open window watching the boys dancing together, chattering and laughing and looking admiringly at him. His one regret was that Moe Lincoln hadn't come. Moe fascinated him, and he kept assuring himself that sooner or later Moe would leave Jacko and come to him.

Freda, a young blond Negro, minced across the room.

"Someone wants you on the phone, dear," he said. "Just wouldn't say who he is."

Toey went into the hall and picked up the receiver. His face brightened with excitement as he recognised Moe's voice.

"Toey," Moe said, "I'm across the way in the Drug Store. I want you over here for five minutes."

"Come on up, baby," Toey said. "Join the party. Come on, baby. You'll have lots of fun."

"I want to talk to you alone," Moe said. "Is Freda there?"

"Yes, but . . ."

"Then you come down here. I don't want him around while I'm talking to you. I've got something to say to you alone."

"You have? What, baby?"

"Jacko and me have had a row. Come on, Toey, for Judas' sake!"

"You mean you two have quarrelled?"

107

"Not a word to anyone. Come on, Toey. I want to talk to you. Hurry it up!"

"I'm coming," Toey said and replaced the receiver. He thought: At last! After all this wait! I'll give him the big front room! I'll have it done over and it'll need a better bed, but . . .

Freda, standing in the doorway, interrupted Toey's thoughts by asking, "Who was that?"

Toey frowned at him. He was bored with Freda now.

"No one you know," he said. "Go back to the party. I don't like being spied on."

Freda gave him a hurt look and returned to the apartment, but as soon as he heard Toey start down the stairs, he silently peered over the banister rail.

He saw Toey reach the dimly lit lobby and make for the front entrance, then he heard Toey give a quick gasp and saw him stumble forward on his hands and knees. Out of the darkness, knife in hand, Moe appeared for a few fleeting, horrible seconds as he thrust the knife twice more into Toey's fat back. Then Moe, like a black ghost, was gone and Freda heard a car start up and drive away. He ran screaming back into the crowded apartment.

The news of Toey Marsh's murder reached police headquarters as Terrell entered the operations room. Two plain clothes officers had Freda with them. Sobbing and moaning, he blurted out to Terrell what he had seen.

"Take him away and lock him up," Terrell said. "Send the wagon out and collect the rest of them. Get Hess with the boys over there. Send out a State alarm for Lincoln."

While this was being dealt with, he drew Beigler aside.

"What the hell's happening in this town?" he said. "Three murders in two days! You know something? I'm scared about that little girl, Angel Prescott. She's the one witness who can pin Henekey's murder on those two. I must be slipping. I should have given her a police guard."

"I'll alert the nearest patrol to go to the motel," Beigler said, reaching for the microphone. "Think it would be an idea to pick her up with her mother and bring them here?"

108

Terrell hesitated, then shook his head.

" Tell them to take them to my home. Carrie will look after them for a couple of days until we find these two hoods. Detail one of the boys to guard the house. Still no news of Jacko?"

" No. Looks as if he's skipped town," Beigler said and started to call the patrol cars. A minute later, he turned to Terrell, " A car will be there in five minutes. They'll take the Prescotts right to your house, Chief."

When Moe reached the Park Motel, he found Hoppy waiting for him.

" A couple of cops took the kid and the woman away about twenty minutes ago," Hoppy reported. " They were in that cabin," and he pointed.

Moe knew then for certain the child had seen Jacko. He cursed, then telling Hoppy to get lost, he drove fast to the nearest drug store and called Lee Hardy's penthouse.

As the telephone bell began to ring, Hardy unlocked his front door and enterd the penthouse. As he walked into the big lounge, he was startled to see Jacko Smith lolling in one of his chairs, the telephone receiver clamped to his fat ear.

Jacko was saying, " Come back here, Moe. Watch it. Dump the car and come in the bus. They know my car," and he hung up.

" What the hell are you doing here?" Hardy said furiously. Jacko eyed him.

" We're in trouble," he said softly. " You, me and Moe. The cops are looking for us."

Gina came to the doorway.

" Tell that fat louse to get out of here!" she screamed. " He forced his filthy . . ."

" Shut up!" Jacko snarled. He looked at Hardy, " It's Henekey."

Hardy lost colour. He turned to Gina. " Look, Pekie, will you wait in the bedroom? I'll handle him."

" I'm going out!" Gina said. " If you imagine I'm going to breathe the same air as this fat slug you're mistaken! You handle him . . . I'm going to a movie!"

"Stay here!" Jacko said viciously as she began to move to the door.

Gina paused and was about to release a stream of abuse when she saw the .38 automatic in his hand, pointing at her. She had been in many difficult situations in her young life, but no one had ever pointed a gun at her before with such glaring, killing eyes behind it. She stared at the gun, not moving.

Hardy said, "Put that gun away!" But there was no real snap in his voice and he looked a little sick.

"She stays here!" Jacko said.

Hardy hesitated, then to Gina, "Better go to your room, Pekie."

"What's the matter with you?" Gina shrilled. "You're not letting this fat slob dictate to you, are you?"

"Get out!" Jacko said and heaved himself out of his chair.

As Hardy made no move to protect her, she turned and ran into her bedroom, slamming the door. Hardy walked over to the cocktail cabinet and poured himself a large Scotch.

"Have you gone nuts, Jacko?" he asked, trying to keep his voice steady. "Put that goddamn gun away!"

Jacko lowered his bulk into the chair. He laid the gun on the broad arm of the chair as he watched Hardy take a drink.

"The cops know we knocked off Henekey," he said. "They've got a witness."

"Damn you!" Hardy exclaimed, his face flushing with rage. "Why weren't you more careful? Who's the witness?"

"A kid. Moe went out to the motel to take care of her, but the cops beat him to it. Toey Marsh saw her fingering me, so Moe slit him. Now we are right in the crap to our necks."

Hardy wiped the cold sweat off his face. He struggled to fight down a rising panic. He said, "Now look, Jacko, you get out of here. From now on, you and Moe are on your own. You're not dragging me into this. You get out!"

Jacko fanned himself with his dirty handkerchief.

"They catch us . . . they catch you. Moe's coming here. We'll sit and wait for him."

Hardy remembered the gun he had in his desk drawer. If he

could kill this fat queer, he could tell the police it was in self-defence. He was sure Gina would back him up and the cops could never hang anything on him with Jacko . . . and Moe, of course, out of the way.

"Well, if you feel that way about it," he said and wandered casually towards his desk. "We'll wait for Moe." He began to open a drawer in his desk when Jacko said, "You want to die, baby? What's it to me to kill a second time? Get away from that desk!"

Hardy looked at the .38 pointing at him, then shrugged and moved away from the desk and sat down.

Moe got off the bus at the Miami terminal. He was now worried. If he couldn't find this kid and knock her off, Jacko and he would be for the gas box. But how to find her? Where had the cops taken her?

He moved quickly through the crowd milling around the terminal and approached the taxi rank. The driver of the first cab was a Jamaican. He nodded to Moe as he opened the cab door. Moe told him to drop him at the beginning of Bay Shore Drive. As the cab moved away, Moe lit a cigarette and tried to relax. He had a ten minute drive ahead of him and he concentrated his thoughts on what his next move should be.

The driver switched on the radio to dance music. As he was approaching Bay Shore Drive, the music faded and the announcer said, "We interrupt this programme for a police message. The police are anxious to question Moe Lincoln, a Jamaican, who they believe can help them with their inquiries concerning the murder of Toey Marsh who was stabbed to death half an hour ago after answering a mysterious telephone call. Lincoln, twenty-three, is tall and thin with a scar from his right ear to his chin. When last seen, he was wearing a white and blue sweat shirt and dark blue jeans. Anyone seeing this man should contact Police Headquarters. Lincoln is known to be dangerous. In no circumstances should anyone attempt to apprehend him. We now return you to Pete Jackson and his Music, playing for you from the Florida Club."

111

The driver snapped off his radio.

" Cops!" he sneered. " They live to make trouble."

Moe slid his knife from its sheath. His heart was hammering. How had the police got onto him so fast? Had someone seen him? He stared intently at the back of the driver's head. He had seen the man stiffen. He was sure he had recognised him from the radio description. So what would he do now?

The driver said scornfully, " Toey Marsh . . . well out of the way! He got me into trouble last month. The guy who slit him did a public service."

Moe relaxed a little.

" Yeah," he said. " I knew him too."

" You want to change your mind about where you want to go?" the driver asked without looking around. " I could run you out of town . . . to Key West. You might fancy getting on a boat. Key West is good for boats."

Moe put his knife away.

" No . . . drop me off here, pal," he said. " This will do fine."

The driver swung to the kerb and Moe paused to look up and down the long road before getting out. He shoved a ten dollar bill at the driver who still didn't look at him, then he walked fast to the nearest alley and disappeared into the darkness.

The driver wiped sweat from his face, then engaging gear, he sent the cab shooting down the road. It took him three minutes to find a patrol officer. Pulling up, he reported where he had dropped Moe.

" You sure it was Lincoln?" the cop demanded.

" I know Lincoln," the driver said, his eyes glittering. " He cut my father once. Man! I thought he was going to cut me, but I played it smart."

The cop climbed into the cab.

" Get me to a telephone."

Five minutes later, two patrol cars pulled up near the alley down which Moe had disappeared. Police spilled out, guns in hand, but they were too late. Although they searched the district, they found no trace of Moe.

The gentle scratching on Lee Hardy's front door alerted Jacko that Moe had arrived. He nodded to Hardy.

" Let him in," he said, lifting the gun so it pointed at Hardy who got to his feet and went into the lobby. As soon as Hardy was out of sight, Jacko went over to the desk and took Hardy's gun from the drawer. He shoved the gun into his hip pocket and then returned to the chair as Moe came into the room, followed by Hardy.

" This caper's turned sour," Moe said and crossing to the cocktail bar, he poured himself a stiff whisky and soda. " It's on the radio. They even know I knocked off Toey."

Hardy said huskily, " You two better get out of here. This is the first place they'll think of to check."

" Shut up!" Jacko snarled. He looked uneasily at Moe. " What do we do, baby?"

" If we can get to Key West, we can get a boat," Moe said, " but we want money."

" He's got money," Jacko said, waving to Hardy. " How much have you got right here?"

" A hundred and fifty," Hardy said. " You can have that."

Moe sneered at him.

" We'll need five grand. We don't stand a prayer without that kind of money."

" I haven't got it."

" You'll find it if you don't want to take a short walk."

Hardy hesitated, then said, " I could get it from the bank tomorrow morning."

Jacko and Moe looked at each other.

" We could stay here for the night," Jacko said.

Moe nodded.

" Yeah, but it's risky."

" We've got to take the risk," Jacko said. To Hardy, he went on, " You get the dough tomorrow morning . . . We'll take care of your girl friend until you get back. You try anything smart and Moe'll slit her."

Listening, her ear against a door panel, Gina flinched, then she silently turned the key in the lock.

Val lay in bed. The moonlight came through the open window and made a square pattern of silver on the carpet.

For the past three hours she had been wrestling with this problem of her husband. What he had said to her during the afternoon had terrified her. She could not believe he had been responsible for this woman's death. This was something she refused to believe. On the floor by her bed lay a mass of newspapers carrying the story of Sue Parnell's murder. She had read everything printed about the murder. On the bedside table lay a writing pad on which she had written the names of the few people connected with the murder and mentioned by the press.

There was this damning evidence of the blood-stained jacket and the cigarette lighter. There was this dreadful thing Chris had said: *One should never pay blackmail. I'll tell the police I did it, and that will be that.* Then he had said: *Last night, I dreamed I killed a woman.*

Val couldn't bear the darkness any longer and sitting up, her face pale, her hands cold and clammy, she turned on the bedside light.

She thought: He didn't do it! I know he didn't. He must have heard about the murder somehow while he was wandering around. Somehow he must have got it into his head that he killed this woman, but I know he didn't! Chris could never do such a thing! Even with those injuries to his brain, he wouldn't do such a thing! It isn't in his nature to stab a woman the way that woman was stabbed!

Then she again thought of the blood-stained jacket. But was it really blood? Was this awful old man getting money out of her by a clever trick? How did she know the stains were from this woman's blood? What to do? She didn't dare go to the police in case . . . She pulled herself together.

She thought: If you really believe Chris didn't do it, then you should go to the police. If you really and truly believe he isn't capable of doing such a terrible thing, then go to Terrell (is that his name?) tell him about this man Hare and let him deal with him.

Then a small, disturbing voice sounded in her mind: But suppose Chris did do it? Just suppose in a moment of mad violence he did kill this woman? Are you going to betray him to the police? Suppose, through you, they were able to prove he did it? Suppose they put him away for life in some awful asylum?

But he didn't do it! Val said, half aloud, her fists clenched, her breath rapid. I know he didn't! This is some trick! I have to find out how this trick was worked! I'm sure it is a trick, but how do I find out? What can I do? She beat her fists together in her agony. I must do something!

Throwing aside the bedclothes, she slid out of bed and began to move restlessly about the room.

It wasn't for nothing that she was the daughter of Charles Travers. She had the same determination, the same fighting spirit as her father. As she moved around the room she became more calm. If she was to help Chris, she must handle this problem herself, she finally decided. Tomorrow, she would pay Hare the money. That would keep him quiet for two weeks. During that time she must somehow try to find out what Chris had been doing while he had lost his memory. If she could find this woman he had met . . . this woman who had made him think of elephants (why elephants?) . . . she might be able to prove he was nowhere near this motel where Sue Parnell had died. If she could do that, then Chris would be safe, but how to find this woman?

She was still pacing the floor, thinking, working herself into a more and more determined frame of mind when the moon faded in the lightening sky and the red rim of the sun began its slow ascent.

115

Chapter Nine

MAX JACOBS watched Val walk into the Florida Banking Corporation. The time was ten minutes past ten. He had been sitting in his car, waiting patiently since nine o'clock. He lit a cigarette and continued to watch and wait. At half-past ten, Val came out of the bank. She was carrying a small brown paper parcel. As she looked up and down the street, Jacobs started the engine. A moment later a taxi drew up at Val's signal and she got into it.

As the cab drew away from the kerb, Jacobs eased his car out of the parking bay and went after it. After a five minute drive, the cab pulled up outside a shabby office block and Val got out.

Jacobs hurriedly parked as Val, paying off the driver, walked into the building. Jacobs risked getting run over as he dodged through the traffic and entered the dark lobby of the building. The elevator was in motion and he started up the stairs, watching the slow crawl of the elevator and seeing it stop on the third floor. He raced to the third floor and arrived, panting. The long corridor with its frosted glass doors was deserted. He leaned against the banister rail, sure that Val had entered one of these offices, and waited.

As Val walked into the outer office of Hare's Investigating Agency, Lucille looked up from her typewriter.

" I have an appointment with Mr. Hare," Val said quietly.

Lucille recognised her. She got to her feet.

" I think he is ready to see you," she said. " Just a moment," and she went into Homer Hare's office, shutting the door.

Hare was nibbling at a bar of chocolate. Sam Karsh stood by the window, smoking. Both men were slightly tense.

"She's here," Lucille said.

The two men looked at each other, then Karsh said, "Are you really going to take her money? Once you take it, we're way out on a limb."

Hare put the chocolate bar reluctantly into his desk drawer.

"Shoo her in," he said to Lucille, then to Karsh, "Run away, Sammy. I'm handling this."

Karsh hesitated, then shrugging, he went out of the office by the door that led into the corridor.

Lucille said, "I hope you know what you're doing. I still don't like it."

Her father grinned as he wiped his sticky fingers on his hand-kerchief.

"But you will. Shoo her in."

Jacobs, watching, had just time to step back out of sight around the bend in the corridor as Karsh appeared. He waited. Karsh stood in the corridor, then moving silently, he entered the outer office as Val walked into Hare's office.

Fifteen minutes later, Val came out of the office and crossed to the elevator. Jacobs saw she no longer was carrying the brown paper parcel. He remained where he was until the ele-vator sank out of sight. Then moving fast, he ran down the stairs, and was in time to see Val leaving the building, walk-ing quickly and heading down-town. He hesitated for a brief moment, then seeing a Drug Store close by, he entered and shut himself in a telephone booth. A minute later, he was talking to Terrell.

"Mrs. Burnett took the money to Homer Hare's Agency," he reported. "She's just left. She was carrying the money done up in a sealed brown paper parcel. She left without it."

This news startled Terrell.

"Homer Hare?" he exclaimed. "You're sure she left the money with him?"

"I'm sure," Jacobs said.

"Okay. Now look, Max, this is important. Get back to the

117

entrance of the office block and stay there. If you see either
Hare, Karsh or his wife leave with the money, pick them up.
Tell them I want to talk to them. Get tough. Don't let them
get rid of the money. Understand?"

"I'll handle it, Chief," Jacobs said and hung up.

Sam Karsh and Lucille came into Hare's office as he tore
open the brown paper parcel. Hare was smiling. The sight of
the hundred dollar bills as they spilt over the desk made Karsh
whistle.

"Wow! That looks good," he said and came close to the desk.
"That looks like real money!"

Hare dug his fingers into the mass of bills, lifted them and let
them flutter back onto the desk.

"Sammy ... we're rich! In two weeks time, the little lady is
going to hand over the rest ... we'll be worth half a million!"

Lucille said, "Stop acting like a miser! What are we going
to do with this right now?"

Hare looked sharply at her.

"What's the matter? You getting an attack of nerves or
something?"

"You're goddamn right I'm getting an attack of nerves!
Suppose the cops walked in now, how would you explain away
this amount of money?"

Hare looked towards Karsh. He smiled his evil smile.

"You married a bright girl, Sammy." He opened a drawer
in his desk and took out a battered brief-case. Quickly he
scooped the money into the case, clipped the case shut and
then pushed it across the desk towards Karsh. "Get moving,
Sammy. Rent a safe at the Miami Safe Deposit. Use any name
that comes to your fertile mind so long as it isn't one of ours
and get moving. The quicker this is salted away, the safer it
will be for us."

Karsh shied away from the case.

"Not me! Lucille can take it. Suppose some cop stops me on
the street? I'm not all that crazy!"

"Take it!" There was a rasp in Hare's voice. "If you want
your cut, you work for it!"

118

Karsh eyed the brief-case, then he looked at his wife who stared blankly at him. He got no encouragement from her, and finally, he picked up the case.

"If I walk into trouble," he said to Hare, "I'll sing like a lark."

"Go ahead and sing," Hare said. "It'll be the last Prima Donna act you'll ever put on!"

Karsh suddenly grinned.

"Forget it! For a third of a half a million, I'd cut my wife's throat."

"And I believe you," Lucille said in a flat, hard voice.

Karsh smiled at her.

"Relax, baby. I was just talking, besides, it'd need a hacksaw to saw through your throat." Tilting his hat over his right eye, he left the office, swinging the brief-case in his hand.

Jacobs, waiting in the lobby, saw Karsh come out of the elevator. He saw the brief-case in his hand. As Karsh walked briskly out onto the street, Jacobs followed him. Karsh got into the office car and searched his pockets for the ignition key. When he found it, and as he was about to sink the key into the ignition lock, Jacobs opened the offside door and slid into the car beside Karsh.

"Hello, peeper," he said and smiled at Karsh who lost colour as he recognised Jacobs. "Headquarters: the Chief wants to talk to you."

Karsh's eyes went furtively to the brief-case that lay on the seat between the two men.

"I'm busy right now," he said. "I'll see him later. What's he want anyway?"

"He didn't tell me," Jacobs said, lighting a cigarette. "Headquarters, Karsh, and snap it up!"

"I tell you, I'm busy right now" Karsh said desperately. "I'm on a job! Get out of my car! I'll see your Chief in half-an-hour. Go on, copper, beat it!"

"You may not know it," Jacobs said, his face suddenly like granite, "but there are some thirty officers, including me, who long to punch you in your left eye. We all think you are the

119

nastiest maggot that crawled out of stinking meat! It would give us all great pleasure to push your horrible eyeball into your horrible brain. I said . . . headquarters!"

"You threatening me?" Karsh said, losing colour.

"That's it, Karsh. I'll give you five seconds to get this car moving. At the end of five seconds, you'll get the sweetest slam in the eye any maggot's ever had."

"I'll fix you," Karsh said breathlessly. He started the car engine. "Don't make any mistake about it! I'll have your badge taken away!"

"If you listen hard enough, maggot, you'll hear my knees knocking," Jacobs said and grinned.

Ten minutes later, Karsh, carrying the brief-case, walked into Terrell's office with Jacobs at his heels.

Terrell looked up from the mass of papers spread out over his desk. Jacobs pointed to the brief-case that Karsh was carrying and nodded his head. This signal went unseen by Karsh as Jacobs was behind him.

"Now listen, Chief," Karsh said furiously, "this punk has no right to take me off a job. He threatened me! I'm going to report him . . ."

Jacobs laced his fingers together, lifted his arms and slammed his hands down on the back of Karsh's neck. Karsh went down on hands and knees, dropping the brief-case. He thought the ceiling had fallen on him. He remained like that until Jacobs planted a solid kick on the seat of his shiny trousers. Karsh staggered to his feet and fell, groaning, into the nearest chair.

"You can't hit a man like that," Terrell said severely, although his eyes were twinkling.

"There was a wasp on his neck, Chief," Jacobs said, looking sad. "I didn't want the poor guy to get stung."

"Is that right?" Terrell said. "For a moment, I thought you were playing rough with him."

"Not me, Chief, you know me," Jacobs said, smiling broadly.

Karsh snarled at him.

"I'll fix you!" he quavered. "You just wait and see."

" There's that wasp again," Terrell said. " Better kill it, Max. Look, it's right on top of the poor guy's head."

As Jacobs, grinning, moved towards Karsh, Karsh scrambled out of the chair and ran across the room, setting his back against the wall.

" Don't touch me!" he yelled frantically. " Leave me alone!"

Terrell looked at Jacobs, then at the brief-case. Jacobs picked up the case, opened it and poured its contents onto the desk.

At this moment the door opened and Beigler came in. At the sight of the money covering the desk, he paused.

" You been robbing a bank, Chief?" he said. " That looks a lot of dough to me."

" It does, doesn't it?" Terrell said. " Let's see just how much there is here."

" Don't touch it!" Karsh exclaimed. " That belongs to Hare! He told me to put it in a safe deposit." Then seeing the three men were staring at him, he went on hurriedly. " It's nothing to do with me! It's Hare's money! I was just . . ."

" Shut up!" Beigler snapped. " You want me to give you a poke in the eye?"

Karsh gulped. He was scared of Beigler. He stood, white and sweating, while Jacobs counted the money.

" Twenty thousand," he said finally.

Terrel leaned back in his chair and regarded Karsh with cold, forbidding eyes.

" Who gave you this money?"

" I told you . . . Hare. He told me to put it in a safe deposit bank. I don't know nothing about it!"

" Yeah? You know Hare hasn't this kind of money. Where did he get it?"

" He didn't tell me. Ask him! Don't ask me!"

" I think the wasp's worrying this punk again," Jacobs said. " Okay for me to swot it?"

" Take him away," Terrell said. " I don't like seeing insects killed. You might tell the boys that Sammy Karsh is here. They'll want to get rid of the wasp with you . . . you mustn't be selfish, Max."

Grinning, Jacobs caught hold of Karsh and locking his arms behind him, he shoved him out of the office. Karsh yelled and struggled, but Jacobs handled him effortlessly. Finally Karsh's yells died away and Terrell looked at Beigler.

"Now what are you going to do?" Beigler said. "That punk mightn't sing."

"I'm going to talk to Homer Hare," Terrell said grimly and reached for the telephone.

As Val walked down Main Street, her mind busy, she became aware of hurrying footfalls behind her . . . tap, tap, tap of high heels, and she glanced around. A girl was coming up behind her, and as Val looked around, the girl smiled hopefully.

"Oh, Mrs. Burnett . . ."

Val stopped and turned.

The girl was shabbily dressed. She wore a grubby white sweater, a skirt that had an oil stain on the front of it, and her shoes were run down. She was around twenty-three, a badly dyed blonde, unattractive and her complexion was bad.

"Oh, Mrs. Burnett, you don't know me, but of course, I know you," the girl said. "I am Mary Sherrek. I know you have never heard of me, but I'm a representative of the *Miami Sun*. It's not much of a paper, but I did so hope . . ." She paused and looked helpless, staring at Val in her neat dress, looking with envy at her perfect grooming. "I don't suppose you want to talk to me but I just had to . . . well, I had to speak to you."

"That's all right," Val said. "What is it?"

"You really mean you don't mind me speaking to you? That's wonderful! You wouldn't give me an interview, would you? I—I—well, I . . ." She stopped and looked uneasily at Val who waited. The girl finally went on, "About your husband . . . he disappeared, didn't he? It would be wonderful for me if you could tell me something about him. You see, I'm not very good at this job and I think they are going to get rid of me. But if I could go back there and give them an exclusive interview with you . . . well, it would . . . you understand?"

While the girl was stammering this out, Val scarcely listened. Her sharp mind was busy. She suddenly saw how it could be possible for her to begin to find out the mystery behind Sue Parnell's death. The idea that had flashed into her mind sent her blood racing excitedly through her body.

"Let's go over there and have a coffee," she said. She led the way across the street and into a cafeteria that was almost empty. She ordered two coffees while Mary Sherrek sat clutching her shabby bag staring at Val with wide, expectant eyes.

"You really mean you will give me an interview, Mrs. Burnett?" she said. "It would save my life. Honest. They are ready to throw me out. If I . . ."

"How long have you been working for this newspaper?" Val asked.

Mary Sherrek looked startled.

"About six months. I got a diploma through a Correspondence College. But I don't think I'm really much good. I just haven't . . ."

"But you have a press card?"

"Oh yes. I couldn't go around without a press card, but it doesn't mean much. It just gets you into places."

"Could I see it, please?"

"Of course."

The girl took the press card from her bag and offered it to Val who studied it for a brief moment. It merely stated that Mary Sherrek represented the *Miami Sun,* and she should be granted facilities to assist her in her work. There was a depressing passport photograph of the girl stuck on the card which was signed by Chief of Police Terrell.

Val put the card on the table.

"Do you want to go home, Mary?"

The girl's eyes opened wide.

"I can't go home. My folk live in New York. I just haven't the money to get there. No, I can't go home."

"If you had the money, would you go?"

123

" Oh yes. I hate it here. Yes, I'd go, but Mrs. Burnett, I should be asking you the questions. You don't want to be bothered with my troubles."

" I want your press card," Val said quietly. " I will give you two hundred dollars for it. With that money you can get home. Will you sell me your press card?"

The girl stared at her as if she thought she had gone out of her mind.

" You can't want my press card! But why? I don't understand."

Val opened her bag and took from it two one hundred dollar bills.

" Never mind why I want it . . . I want it. Here's the money. Can I take the card?"

Mary Sherrek stared at the two bills. She drew in a deep breath.

" You really mean it?"

" Here is the money," Val said, trying to control her impatience. She pushed the money across the table and picked up the card. This she put in her bag. " Now go home. I get these odd whims. I like to help people. Good luck . . ." She got to her feet as the girl continued to stare at the two bills on the table. Then she walked quickly from the cafeteria.

A passing taxi stopped at her signal. As she got into the cab, she looked back. The girl was coming out of the cafeteria, looking bewildered, but happy.

Val gave the driver the address of her hotel. As the cab moved off, she took the press card from her bag and studied it. Back at the hotel, she had a spare passport photograph of herself. This she could easily stick on the card. Armed with this authority, she now had a remote chance of finding out more about Sue Parnell's murder.

Homer Hare strode into Terrell's office like a fat Avenging Angel. He met Terrell and Beigler's bleak stares with a stare even more bleak.

" Where's my son-in-law?" he demanded, coming to rest

124

before Terrell's desk. "If you've so much as laid a finger on him, I'm going to my attorney. Where is he?"

Terrell slapped the brief-case lying on his desk.

"Who gave you this money?" he demanded in his Cop voice.

"I'll answer questions when you answer mine!" Hare rumbled. "Don't you think you can scare me! I know my rights! Where's Karsh?"

"He'll be along," Terrell said. "Where did you get this money from?"

"That's my business." Hare lowered his bulk into a chair. "I want him right here and now! unless you produce him, I'm not talking."

Terrell nodded to Beigler who left the office. Terrell and Hare regarded each other.

"I didn't think you were this much of a fool," Terrell said. "You've been in your racket now for over thirty years. You've done pretty well. You haven't been entirely honest, but you've kept within the line. Blackmail isn't a pretty thing, Hare. I'd have thought you'd have been smart enough to resist that temptation."

Hare glared at him.

"I haven't an idea what you're talking about," he said. "You be careful! Blackmail! You're lucky there are no witnesses!"

The door opened and Beigler came in, shoving Karsh before him. Karsh had a black eye and was sweating and shaking.

Terrell stared at him in apparent astonishment.

"What happened to him then? How did he get that shiner?"

Beigler shook his head sadly.

"I guess he's born clumsy. He fell over his feet and took a toss down the stairs. But he's all right now, aren't you, Shamus?"

Karsh shied away from him. He held his hand to his eye and groaned.

"Sit him down," Terrell said. "He looks in need of a rest."

Beigler slammed a chair behind Karsh's knees and he sat down violently.

"Are you all right, Sammy?" Hare asked, staring at him.

125

"Do I look all right?" Karsh snarled, mopping his eye with his handkerchief.

"Hare!" Terrell barked, "where did you get this money from?"

Hare leaned against the chair back making it creak.

"It's a retainer. An important client. No business of yours."

"I happen to know who your client is," Terrell said. "This a retainer? Twenty thousand dollars? Come on, spill it, what's it all about?"

Hare smiled calmly.

"You must ask my client," he said. "I was paid this amount for services to be rendered. It's not police business . . . strictly private business. If you do know who my client is, then ask my client." He got to his feet and picked up the brief-case. "One little thing, Chief, if you know who my client is, you'll also know you'll have to watch your step very carefully. My client draws lots of water in this town. You could be on the retired list if you play the wrong card. Come on, Sammy. They can't hold us. Let's go."

"Just a moment," Terrell said, his hands in fists on the desk. "You're having a run, Hare, but it won't last. From now on, I'm out to get you."

Hare winked.

"You try. You won't get me. I'm strictly honest."

"And another thing," Terrell said. "I have the numbers of those bills. You spend one of them and you'll be in trouble."

"Think so? You talk to my client," Hare said and stumped out of the office, followed by Karsh.

Terrell and Beigler exchanged glances.

"Well, I didn't play that one too smart," Terrell said, frowning. "I thought he just might crack."

"Hare? Crack?" Beigler snorted. "So what do we do now?"

Terrell reached for the telephone.

"Get me the Spanish Bay hotel. I want to talk to Mrs. Val Burnett," he said to the police operator.

A few minutes later, the operator told him Mrs. Burnett was out.

Replacing the receiver Terrell shrugged.

" I'll leave this to you, Joe," he said. " I want to talk to her as soon as she gets back to the hotel, but let's handle it carefully. Don't let's make a thing of it."

" What can Hare have on her . . . a woman like that?" Beigler said, scowling. " Twenty thousand! What's she been up to that he's managed to throw that size hook into her?"

" That's what I want to find out," Terrell said. He looked at the papers on his desk. " We seem to be getting nowhere fast with the Parnell killing. What are you doing about it Joe?"

Exasperated, Beigler began to explain when the telephone bell rang.

Terrell listened to the excited voice coming over the line and Beigler saw his face harden.

" We'll be right over," he said. " Don't touch anything," and he hung up. He stared at Beigler. " Spike Calder's been found in a cellar room in his club. Been dead sometime."

Beigler groaned.

" What's the matter with this town? Okay, I'm on my way."

" Could be Lincoln again," Terrell said. " He and Calder knew each other. Calder was stabbed. Could be where Jacko and Lincoln have been hiding out."

Beigler nodded and ran from the office.

Joan Parnell sprawled in the big shabby armchair, a black cat on her lap, a glass of gin and water in her hand. She stared glassily at Val who sat on the edge of her chair, a newly bought notebook in her lap, a fountain pen in her hand.

She had been careful to put on a simple grey dress. She wore no stockings and she had removed the varnish from her nails. As an afterthought she had slightly disarranged her usually immaculate hair, but even with these touches, she felt she didn't look much like a reporter from the *Miami Sun*.

She realised with relief that Joan Parnell was so drunk, she need not have taken any care. The sight of this handsome woman, her face white, her eyes peering as if to focus her properly, her hand unsteady as she held her glass upset Val.

" The *Miami Sun*?" Joan said thickly. " That's just a rag. What do you want?"

" It's about your sister," Val said, speaking slowly and quietly. " My Editor thinks you aren't getting much help from the police. He has taken an interest in the case. The police don't seem to be getting anywhere and he thought if you could give me some information, we might spotlight the case and get the police to take more interest."

" Do you imagine I need the help of a rag like the *Miami Sun*?" Joan said. " I'll tell you something : I knew the police wouldn't do a thing. I'll tell you why : my sister was a whore. The police couldn't care less about whores. I'll tell you what I've done. I've gone to the best detective agency in this rotten town and I have paid them good money to find out who killed my sister. Tell that to your Editor !"

" Would that be Hare's Investigating Agency?"

" Who else? I said the best, didn't I? And when they find the man who killed my sister, that fool Terrell is going to look damned small !"

Val's mind moved swiftly. It became obvious to her that Hare was now double-crossing this woman so he could blackmail Val herself. He had found out something that the police knew nothing about and instead of telling this woman, he had come to her with this blackmail proposition.

" Have you heard from the Agency yet?" Val asked.

" Not yet. I'm giving them a little time. I'll hear . . . they're smart."

" I see." Val pretended to write something in her notebook. " But perhaps you have your own idea who killed your sister, Miss Parnell? This, of course, would be off the record."

" There is one bastard who could have done it," Joan said, brushing the cat off her lap and sitting upright. " That's Lee Hardy. He threw her out and is shacked up with a pug faced bitch who calls herself Gina Lang. I'll tell you something : Sue wouldn't stand for any man throwing her out. It's my bet she made trouble for that heel and he's fixed her. I told that fool Terrell, but he wouldn't listen. You go and talk to Hardy. You can tell him from me, I think he did it! Now get out of here!"

"Where do I find him?" Val asked, writing the name in her book.

"Oh, in the phone book," Joan said impatiently and got unsteadily to her feet. "You tell your Editor I'm going to find the man who killed my sister! I can do without the help of his rotten rag!"

As Val got into the waiting taxi and told the driver to take her to the nearest drug store, Lee Hardy sat in his office counting the money he had finally raised for Jacko and Moe's getaway stake. He had had considerable difficulty in raising five thousand dollars. His bank account was overdrawn and the manager had flatly refused him further credit. He had had to go around to several of his bookmaker pals and talk them into advancing sums until the sums totalled five thousand dollars.

He put the money in a brief-case and telling his girl he wouldn't be back until the following morning, he left the office. It was a few minutes after midday when he reached his apartment. He had been worrying about leaving Gina alone with these two thugs. He didn't trust them even after the payoff. He had borrowed a .45 automatic from one of his friends and this he now carried in his hip pocket. He felt a lot more sure of himself now he had the gun.

If Jacko and Moe managed to leave town, they all might escape this rap, he was thinking as he paid off the taxi driver, but the chances of them getting clear wasn't so good. The police were now alerted. Jacko was as easy to recognise as an elephant.

Hardy knew he was in serious trouble. If the police caught these two, they would sing. They would implicate him the moment the cuffs were on their wrists. If he was to get out of this jam he would have to silence them both. As the elevator took him up to his penthouse, he decided he would have to alert the police the moment Jacko and Moe left. He would Get Gina to do this. He would kill them both before they reached the street. He would then fire Jacko's gun two or three times into his front door to prove to the police these two turned on him and had tried to kill him. Terrell wouldn't be able to prove otherwise. The fact Gina had called the police should get him out of this jam.

The elevator came to a sighing stop on the top floor of the apartment block. The doors swung open. As Hardy stepped out into the wide corridor, he saw a tall, slimly built girl move through the open doorway of his penthouse : the door opened by Gina.

Hardy walked quickly across the corridor, catching Gina's eye. He was in time to hear the slim girl say, " I am Mary Sherrek. I am from the *Miami Sun.* Could I see Mr. Hardy?"

Gina, her face tense, said, " He's right behind you. I'm sure he'd love to talk to you."

The girl turned. Hardy was struck by her beauty, but immediately became uneasy by the expression in her eyes. The steady, searching look threw him off balance.

He switched on his charm as he entered the penthouse and closed the door. Gina moved into the lounge.

" The *Miami Sun?* " Hardy said, his voice a shade too hearty. " Why, sure. I read it every day. What do you want? But come on in." He entered the lounge and looked questioningly at Gina. She gave a slight nod, indicating that Jacko and Moe were in Hardy's bedroom. He was quick to see the door was ajar.

Val looked around the lounge. There was a highly charged atmosphere that scared her. Both this girl, wearing lounging pyjamas and this big handsome man, seemed very on edge.

" Sit down, sit down, sit down," Hardy said waving to a chair. " Just what's on your mind, Miss . . . what did you say your name is?"

" Sherrek," Val said, sitting down, clutching her notebook and trying to control the thumping of her heart.

" Well, Miss Sherrek, I'm pretty busy. Just what is it?" Hardy said. He put the brief-case containing the five thousand dollars on the settee. " How about a drink?"

" No, thank you."

" Get me a drink, Pekie," Hardy said. " I have a thirst that would slay a camel. Now what is it?" he went on to Val as Gina moved to the cocktail cabinet.

Val really wasn't sure how to handle this situation. She knew it could be dangerous. She knew there was something going on in the penthouse that these two didn't want her to know about. She had seen Gina's nod to a door leading from the lounge. She was sure it was some signal to Hardy.

" I'm covering the Parnell murder," she said. " I understand you were a friend of Miss Parnell. I wonder if you could tell me about her . . . give me something of her background and whether you have any ideas who could have murdered her."

Hardy sat down. His face became granite hard and his eyes vicious.

" I'm not talking about her," he said. " She's dead now. I know nothing about who killed her or why she was killed."

Gina came across the room, swinging her neat hips, carrying a large glass of whisky and ice. As she offered Hardy the glass, she said spitefully, " She was just an old, old flame that flickered out . . . a nobody . . . a tart."

Val scarcely heard what she was saying. She was staring with rooted concentration, feeling a chill crawling up her spine, at the heavy gold bracelet around Gina's slim wrist. From the bracelet hung a cluster of five miniature gold elephants.

Chapter Ten

THE POLICE search for Jacko and Moe had been intensified. Every officer that Terrell could spare was now thrown into the hunt. Somewhat late in the day, road blocks were set up.

Officers Tom Lepski and Bill Williams were told to go to Lee Hardy's penthouse.

Beigler said, " You won't find those two hoods there, but they might have been there. Get rough with that pug-faced girl. She might have seen something. Put pressure on Hardy. He could have staked them to get rid of them. Check his bank. See if he has made a big withdrawal yesterday or today."

" We'll go to the bank first," Lepski said to Williams as they got into their car. " I'd like to have a few facts to ram down Hardy's throat."

Williams, a tall, youngish man who spent most of his time in the finger-print department was resentful that he should have been taken from his safe desk and teamed with a crazy man like Lepski. He was sure Lepski could lead him into trouble. The thought of suddenly being confronted by two such vicious thugs as Jacko and Moe scared him. It was all very well for Lepski who had had years of experience handling thugs. He was unmarried and as reckless as a madman. Williams up to now had managed to keep clear of violence. Besides, his wife was expecting their third baby. What would happen to her if he got killed?

Lepski, wiry, tough, his sun-tanned face lined and his clear blue eyes alert, drove the police car swiftly to the Commercial and South Banking Corporation where he knew Hardy banked.

" What's the matter with you?" he demanded, as he weaved the car expertly through the heavy traffic. " You look like you swallowed a bee."

Williams shifted uneasily.

" There's nothing the matter with me," he said shortly. He couldn't admit he was sick with fear. That kind of confession might get back to Terrell.

Lepski poked his head out of the car window and cursed a driver who was trying to cut in. The driver started to curse back, then seeing the black and white stripe on the car with the word POLICE on the hood, he hurriedly bit back his angry words.

Lepski sneered at him, then turned his attention once more to Williams.

" Relax. You can only die once. I'd rather get a slug in the gut than cancer."

Williams flinched. He shifted lower in the car seat. His hot, sweating hand moved inside his coat and touched the butt of his .38. The feel of the cold metal gave him no comfort.

Parking, the two men walked into the bank and after a brief wait, they were shown into the manager's office.

The manager, lean and balding, was one of the best .22 rifle shots in Miami. He had shot against Lepski often enough and Lepski was one of the few members of the rifle club who could match him. He beamed as he shook hands.

" I'll be at the club tonight," he said. " I have a pal coming who can shoot nearly as good as I can. Will you be there, Tom?"

" I guess not," Lepski said regretfully. " I have a murder hunt in my hair. If I can, I will if only to show your pal a trick or two."

The manager whose name was Werner, laughed.

" What's this murder hunt, Tom?"

" A couple of hoods. Look, you could help. I don't expect you to give bank secrets away, but this is important. Has Lee Hardy asked you for money . . . today or yesterday?"

" Now, Tom, you know that's not a proper question to ask."

"Yeah, but we have reason to believe Hardy could have staked these two for a quick getaway. They are his men. So far they have murdered three not-so-important people. If we don't find them fast, they could murder others . . . more important."

Werner looked shocked. He hesitated, then said, "All I can tell you is a certain party came here and wanted five thousand dollars. He was in the red, and I wouldn't give him credit. He was here around ten o'clock this morning."

"Thanks," Lepski said. "Maybe I will be seeing you at the club tonight after all."

When they got back to their car, Lepski said, "Now we'll go talk to Hardy."

"Think it would be an idea to call the Chief?" Williams asked without much hope. "Maybe he would want to talk to Hardy himself."

"We go talk to Hardy," Lepski repeated and started the car. As he moved the car into the stream of traffic he went on, "How are you with a gun, Bill?"

"Not so good," Williams said, sweat on his face. "I haven't been to the range for a couple of years. You know, Tom, this is beginning to bother me. Suppose we walk into those two?"

"What two?" Lepski asked. "You mean Jacko and Moe? So what? They either come quietly or they come dead. Even if you are a lousy shot you couldn't miss a fat slob as big as Jacko. Shoot him in the gut . . . that'll let the gas out of him!"

"Those two are pretty handy with a gun themselves," Williams said miserably. "My wife is expecting a baby."

"Is that right? Well, so long as you don't have the baby, why should you worry?" Lepski said and swinging the car into a parking bay, he switched off the ignition. "Come on : let's go talk to Hardy."

The two men walked down the street until they came to Hardy's apartment block. Nearby, Lepski spotted a patrol officer. He signalled to him. The officer hurried up.

"Look, Jamey, I'm going to talk to Lee Hardy. I don't expect trouble, but I could walk into it. If you hear guns, get the boys. Understand? Don't come up and be a hero : get the boys. Then get back here and pop those two if they come out . . . we're after Jacko and Moe."

That seemed to make sense to the officer and Williams, who was now feeling pretty sick, envied him.

"Okay. There's a call booth at the end of the road," the officer said. "I hear shooting and I'll be in there faster than a Sputnik."

Lepski sneered at him, then nodding to Williams, he walked into the apartment block.

The porter, standing behind the big desk, eyed him suspiciously. He recognised him as a cop.

"Seen Mr. Hardy go up?" Lepski asked.

"He went up five minutes ago," the porter said. "If you want him, I'll call him."

"No you don't," Lepski said, giving the porter a hard stare. "Keep your paws off the telephone or I'll make your future life a misery."

Then again nodding to Williams, he went across the lobby and entered the elevator. As they ascended to the top floor, Williams said, "So what do we do now?"

"I'm not expecting trouble," Lepski said. "Hardy wouldn't be such a mug as to hide those two in his place. I ring on the bell and walk in. You keep out of sight, against the wall. If trouble starts, then come in shooting, but for God's sake make sure you don't shoot me. Get it?"

Williams said he got it.

The elevator came to a halt opposite Hardy's ornate front door. Lepski and Williams moved out into the wide corridor. Lepski showed Williams where he should stand. He winked at him.

"Don't lay an egg," he said. "This should be an easy one."

Williams watched him step up to the front door and ring the bell. He had to admire Lepski's cool courage. He was no more ruffled than if he were calling on a Mormon Bishop.

There was a pause, then the door opened and Gina stood

there. Lepski could see into the lounge. Hardy and a tall, slim girl were staring towards him. He didn't hesitate. He walked forward, riding Gina out of his way.

"Hey! Who are you?" Gina said shrilly. "What . . . ?"

But by then Lepski had entered the lounge. He and Hardy looked at each other. Hardy knew Lepski and he lost colour.

"What do you mean busting in like this?" he blustered. "I'm busy. What is it?"

Lepski was now looking at Val with puzzled probing eyes. Where had he seen this girl before? he asked himself. Who was she?

"Take it easy," he said to Hardy. "I don't know your girl friend. Show some manners. Introduce me."

"When I want you in my place, I'll invite you," Hardy snarled. "You . . ."

"I said introduce me, boy."

Gina came in.

"This is Mary Sherrek of the *Miami Sun*," she said.

Lepski knew Mary Sherrek well. She often bothered him, trying to get information. He looked steadily at Val who faced him, her eyes big, her body tense.

"Is that right? I'm Detective Officer Tom Lepski. Always glad to meet the press."

"Miss Sherrek is leaving," Gina said.

"Not right now." Lepski moved so he could watch the three of them. "She could have a nice little story for her paper. I'm great at giving press hand-outs. Stick around, sister. Get your little book ready."

Hardy said, "Just what do you want?"

"Jacko and Moe. Where are they?"

"Why ask me? I don't know."

Lepski spotted the brief-case lying on the settee.

"The Chief thinks otherwise. Those two are wanted for three murders. Now's the time to flap with your mouth or you can get caught with an accessory rap."

Hardy hesitated. He was horribly aware that Jacko and Moe, in the bedroom, were listening.

" I tell you I haven't seen them for a couple of days," he said finally.

" Too bad . . . for you," Lepski said and moved quickly to the brief-case, picked it up, snapped open the lock and emptied its contents on the settee.

Hardy cursed and moved towards Lepski who turned and grinned savagely at him.

" Want a poke in the kisser, Hardy?" he asked. " What's all this money for?"

" It's betting money," Hardy said. " Now, get out of here!"

" I guess I'll look the joint over before I go," Lepski said. " Just in case . . ."

" Not without a warrant!"

" I can get one, but I'll look now."

" You do it and I'll see you lose your badge," Hardy said. " I mean just that!"

Lepski knew he could get into trouble if he searched the penthouse without a warrant. Hardy had connections with people important enough to put him in Dutch.

" Then I'll get a warrant. I have a couple of men outside. Why waste time, if you have nothing to hide?"

" Get out of here!" Hardy repeated.

Lepski shrugged.

" Okay, but I'll be back." He started towards the door. " Remember! there are two of my men outside. You stay right here until I get back." As he passed Val, he took a firm grip on her arm. " Let's go, Miss Sherrek. I have a story for you."

Hardy and Gina stood motionless, watching Lepski lead Val out of the penthouse. Lepski closed the door behind him.

Williams, sweat beading his face, drew in a long slow breath of relief at the sight of Lepski.

" Okay?" he asked, staring at Val.

" I don't know. You stick here," Lepski said. " Don't let anyone out. I'm getting a warrant. If anyone tries to leave, get tough. Me and the little lady are going to headquarters. You'll have the boys with you in ten minutes."

Williams gulped.

" Ten minutes?"

Lepski moved Val to the elevator.

" That's what the man said." He nodded and thumbed the button. The doors swished to and the elevator began its smooth descent.

" Just who are you?" Lepski said staring at Val with his hard Cop's eyes. " You're not Mary Sherrek. I know her . . . so who are you?"

" There was a mistake," Val said, fighting her panic. " That man thought I was Miss Sherrek."

" You don't work for the *Miami Sun*. I know all the dopes on that rag," Lepski said. " You'll have to come to headquarters, baby. The Chief will want to talk to you."

Val controlled the urge to run. She stiffened and gave Lepski a cold stare.

" If you must know : I am Mrs. Valerie Burnett. My father is Charles Travers. You may have heard of him. I am not going with you !"

Lepski recognised her then. He felt as if he had stepped on the teeth of a rake and had the rake handle slam him in the face.

" I didn't know," he said sure Terrell would skin him if he caused trouble with the daughter of Charles Travers. " I'm sorry."

Val forced a smile.

" It's all right," she said and walked quickly out of the lobby. Lepski followed more slowly. He saw her wave to a taxi, get in and the cab drive away. The Patrol Officer joined him.

" Stick right here," Lepski said. " There could be trouble. Williams is up there. I'm getting a search warrant. Watch it !"

Leaving the Patrol Officer staring after him, Lepski sprinted for his car.

Jacko came out of the bedroom. His fat face was running with sweat : his mean little eyes vicious.

" Let's have the money," he said. " We're off !"

"You heard what he said," Hardy exclaimed. "You can't go that way. There are cops out there!"

Moe slid into the room.

"No cop is stopping us," he said. "Let's have the dough."

"You can't do it!" Hardy said, trying to control the quaver in his voice. "You start shooting and they'll know I've been hiding you. We've got to think . . ."

"Shut up!" Jacko snarled. He waddled over to the settee and began cramming the money into the brief-case. He snapped the case shut, then took Hardy's gun from his hip pocket and gave it to Moe.

"Now, wait . . . for God's sake!" Hardy said.

"The girl . . ." Jacko jerked his head at Gina.

"You leave her alone . . ." Hardy began when Moe reached him. Moe hit him on the side of the head with his gun barrel. Hardy went down on hands and knees.

As Gina opened her mouth to scream, Jacko dug a hard fat finger into her stomach. She jack-knifed forward, gasping. He grabbed her and shook her viciously. The smell of stale sweat coming from him sickened her.

"Shut up!" he said. "You go out there and talk to the cops. You make one false move and you'll get a second navel! Out!"

He gave her a shove towards the door. She staggered, recovered her balance, then under the threat of Jacko's gun, crossed the lobby. Jacko and Moe followed her. Jacko motioned her to open the front door. She hesitated, then opening the door, she stepped into the corridor.

Williams, gun in hand gaped at her. Sweat beaded his face, his mouth was dry. He was scared out of his wits.

Gina stood staring at him.

"Get back!" Williams said. "You stay right in there . . . go on . . . get back!"

Then Moe like an evil black ghost, slid around the doorway and his gun spat flame.

Williams didn't even see him. He felt a shocking thump in the middle of his chest and the gun slipped out of his hand. He went down, his face scraping along the lush carpet of the corridor. He came to rest at Gina's feet. For a long moment, he twisted and turned, then he became still. Gina clapped her hands across her mouth and backed away from Moe who came further out into the corridor, his black eyes rolling, his mouth a vicious line. He paused to make certain there was no other cop in the corridor, then he moved into the elevator. Jacko came waddling out, carrying the brief-case. He was panting, his face ashen. He threw himself into the elevator as Moe groped for the button.

Hardy, rolling on his side, looked through the open doors of the lounge and the front door. He saw Jacko's massive body against the grill of the elevator. He pulled his borrowed gun from his hip pocket and fired in one lightening movement. The gun exploded as the elevator doors swished shut.

Falling on her knees, Gina began to scream.

Moe heard the shot and saw Jacko heave back. He watched with horrified eyes the great mountain of fat slowly collapse like a stricken elephant. He saw the splash of blood below Jacko's left hand shirt pocket. He didn't have to touch Jacko to know that Hardy had killed him. Shuddering, his black face glistening with sweat, his lips drawn off his teeth. Moe snatched up the brief-case.

As the elevator came to rest and the doors swung open, Patrol Officer Jamey, gun in hand, came rushing blindly into the lobby. The two men fired simultaneously. Jamey's slug nicked Moe's left ear. Moe's slug took Jamey squarely between the eyes. Jamey went down like a pole-axed bull.

The sound of the shooting brought people out onto the street. Cars stopped. Two or three women began to scream.

Moe, panting, ran down the corridor to the basement stairs. The janitor, poking his head out of his office, saw him, gave a smothered yell and threw himself flat on the floor. Moe swept past him and down the stairs.

Cursing, Moe blundered along a dimly lit corridor as the approaching sound of Police sirens added to his panic. He reached a door, pulled back two bolts, dragged the door open and stepped into hot sunshine and a narrow alley that led to the waterfront. He ran down the alley, paused at the end of it and looked back. There was a woman leaning out of a window in the apartment block, staring down at him: a fat, middle-aged woman with blue dyed hair. As she saw him look at her, she started back and began to scream.

Moe shoved the gun into the waistband of his jeans and walked quickly along the waterfront. Within fifty yards was Fris-Fris's bar. Fris-Fris had once been Moe's lover. He was a fat, elderly Jamaican, a reefer addict, who made a reasonable living organising a Call-boy service for the degenerate rich of Miami.

Moe entered the dark little bar. At this hour, only Fris-Fris was in the bar. He was dozing behind the counter, a sporting sheet spread out before him, a cup of cold coffee near at hand.

Moe grabbed his arm.

"Fris! Get me under cover! The cops are after me!"

Fris-Fris sprang out of his daydreams. He moved with the smoothness of a snake. Holding Moe's arm, he drew him into a room at the back of the bar, pulled aside a curtain, shoved Moe into another room where a man slept on a straw mattress, past the sleeping man and into a narrow corridor.

Fris-Fris fiddled with a hidden catch: a panel that looked like a continuation of the wooden wall slid back and he shoved Moe into a small recess.

"Wait, I'll fix it," he said and closed the panel.

He scurried back to the bar, settled himself and closed his eyes. A minute later, two patrol officers came in. One of them reached across the bar and slapped Fris-Fris across his fat face.

"Wake up, Queen," the officer barked. "Where's Moe Lincoln?"

Fris-Fris blinked the tears out of his eyes.

"Lincoln? I haven't seen him in weeks."

The two officers, guns in hands, went through the sordid little building, but they didn't find Moe.

While the hunt for Moe was going on, the news of Williams's death was flashed to police headquarters.

Terrell and Beigler bundled into a police car and rushed over to Hardy's penthouse. Lepski was already there.

Hardy lay on the settee. A livid bruise from Moe's gun showed on his white face. Gina, sick looking, her eyes dark with fear, sat in an armchair, sipping whisky.

Lepski was prowling around the room, jumpy and ready to hit out at anyone.

As Terrell and Beigler entered the apartment block, four white coated interns staggered out, carrying Jacko's gross body on a stretcher. Terrell stared at the vast mound of flesh, hidden under the sheet, grunted and then walked with Beigler to the elevator.

"This slob was hiding them," Lepski said as Terrell and Beigler came into the penthouse. "I don't give a damn what he says . . . he was hiding them!"

"Okay," Terrell said. "Get after Lincoln, Tom. I'll handle this."

Lepski snarled at Hardy who had slowly sat up. Then he walked out of the lounge.

Hardy knew as he met Terrell's cold, hostile eyes, that this was his moment of truth. He had either to play his cards right or he would land in the gas chamber.

"Chief . . . they came here last night," he said. "Jacko and Moe. I was out. They settled in: threatening Miss Lang. When I came in, they told me they had knocked off Henekey. He had double-crossed them in some deal. They didn't say what. They wanted a getaway stake . . . five thousand. At first, I wouldn't play, but they had me. They said if I didn't give them the money, they would crucify Gina . . . Miss Lang. Those were Jacko's very words. When that hood promises to do something like that . . . he does it. So I got the money. Then Lepski came here. Those two were in the bedroom. They heard Lepski tell me there was an officer outside. When Lepski left, they forced Gina to go out there and talk to the officer, then Moe went out and killed him." Dramatically, Hardy tossed his .45 automatic on the table. "I killed Jacko. I admit it. When I heard the shooting, I grabbed my gun and fired at him as he got into the elevator."

"All right," Terrell said curtly. "Let's start again." He looked at Beigler. "Let's have it down in writing."

It was a little after five o'clock that evening that Terrell heard from Lepski that he had met Val Burnett in Hardy's penthouse and that she had been there representing the *Miami Sun*.

Terrell was both tired and worried. Moe Lincoln had again slipped through the police drag-net. Terrell had arrested Lee Hardy for killing Jacko, but Hardy's lawyer had got Hardy out of the hands of the police on bail. Hardy had claimed he had been forced to kill Jacko as Jacko was about to shoot Gina. As Gina supported this story, there was nothing Terrell could do but to allow Hardy out on bail.

At first he couldn't believe that Val Burnett had masqueraded as a press reporter, but when Lepski had finally convinced him, he got in his car and drove fast to the Spanish Bay hotel.

Val received him in the sitting-room of her suite.

" I'm sorry to disturb you, Mrs. Burnett," Terrell said as he came into the room. " I understand from one of my officers that you were in Hardy's penthouse a few minutes before this shooting affair."

Val, who had been expecting this call, had prepared her story, and although she was tense, she faced Terrell calmly enough.

"Yes, I was there. It was very stupid of me," she said. "Do sit down. Of course you want an explanation."

Terrell sat down.

" I understand you told Hardy you were Mary Sherrek of the *Miami Sun*, Mrs. Burnett. Is that correct?"

Val sat down, facing Terrell.

"Yes. It was like this : Miss Sherrek wanted to go home. She was short of money. I was sorry for her so I bought her press card. I suppose I had no right to do it, but I wanted an excuse to help her and I also wanted to amuse myself."

" She had no right to sell the card to you," Terrell said sharply. " I don't understand : just why did you buy it?"

" Oh, a sudden impulse." Val made a vague gesture with her hands. " I suppose it is difficult for you to understand my position. I am wealthy. I have nothing to do. I have always been

fascinated by crime." She forced a smile. " This woman's murder
. . . Sue Parnell . . . more than interested me. I've followed the
case in the papers. It suddenly occurred to me while I was talking to the girl it would be amusing and interesting to meet some
of the people connected with the case. I realised if I had a press
card, I could go to these people's homes and talk to them. So I
just couldn't resist the temptation and I bought the card from
this girl. I called on Mr. Hardy. You'll probably think this is
rather morbid, but people like myself who have too much money
and not enough to do, do these things for—for kicks."

Terrell stared at her. He didn't believe a word she was saying,
but he had to be careful.

" It was a very foolish and dangerous thing to have done, Mrs.
Burnett," he said finally.

"Yes, wasn't it? Well, I'm sorry if I have caused trouble.
Perhaps you will be kind enough to write it off as a silly, rich
woman's whim."

Terrell wasn't to be taken in by this kind of humility.

" When you were in the penthouse," he said, " had you any
idea these two killers were there?"

" Oh, of course not!"

" Could I have Sherrek's press card, please?"

Val stiffened, then stared steadily at him.

" I hope you're not going to make trouble for the girl," she
said. " I wouldn't like that. All this is entirely my fault.
I destroyed the card when I got back here."

Terrell shifted ground.

" There's another thing, Mrs. Burnett. It has come to my
knowledge that you have given Homer Hare twenty thousand
dollars. He claims it is a retainer for work to be done. I admit
this isn't my business, but I feel it is my duty to warn you that
Hare is thoroughly unreliable and thoroughly dishonest." He
hesitated, then went on, " On the face of it, Mrs. Burnett, it
seems to me that Hare might be blackmailing you. Nothing
would please me more than to put him away for fourteen years.
Anything you wish to tell me that would enable me to get a
conviction against him would be in the strictest confidence. I

144

assure you of that." He paused, then went on. " Is there anything you would care to tell me?"

Val felt cold. She sat for a long moment staring at Terrell, then she said, " I gave this man the money because I want him to do certain very confidential work for me. There is no question of blackmail." She got to her feet. " Thank you for your offer of help, but it is quite unnecessary. Please accept my apologies for my foolishness."

Terrell shrugged and stood up.

" All right, Mrs. Burnett, but if you change your mind, you know where to find me. If I can be of help, let me know." He moved to the door, then pausing, he said, " I'm sorry, but this isn't the end of the matter. Hardy is coming up on a manslaughter charge. He could call you as a witness. I'm not satisfied you have told me the truth. Think about it. People have found it is better to have me on their side than against them."

He went out and shut the door quietly behind him.

The time was seven-fifteen. Homer Hare, Sam Karsh and Lucille were in conference. Sam Karsh had just got back from hospital where he had been treated for bruises and shock. It had taken him more than seven hours to recover enough from the police beating to get back to the office. Even now, he held an ice-bag to his aching eye and he moaned now and then. Neither Hare, who was munching chicken sandwiches, nor Lucille paid any attention to him.

" I said from the beginning I didn't like it," Lucille said, " and now this."

" Terrell's bluffing," Hare said, his mouth full. " He can't prove the money isn't a retainer. The Burnett woman won't talk. There's nothing to worry about.

" Yeah?" Karsh whined. " How about me? Look at the way those Nazis beat me up! Know what they said? They said every time they see me in the car, they will frame me for a traffic violation and they'll do it! Look at my eye!"

" Oh shut up about your damned eye!" Lucille exclaimed shrilly. " Who cares? I think . . ."

The buzzer sounded in the outer office. The three of them looked uneasily at each other. Then Lucille got to her feet and was moving to the door when it opened. Even Hare was startled to see Val standing in the doorway. With an effort, he switched on his oily smile and got to his feet. He bowed elaborately.

"Mrs. Burnett: I am honoured. Please come in."

Val looked from him to Lucille and then to Karsh who hurriedly hid the ice-bag behind him and stared at her uneasily.

"All right, children," Hare said smoothly. "Run along. Mrs. Burnett doesn't want you here."

"But I do," Val said with quiet determination. She moved further into the office and closed the door. She was pale but there was an expression in her eyes and a hardness around her mouth that made Hare look sharply at her. "I think your two assistants know you are blackmailing me."

Karsh flinched and turned a putty white. Even Lucille, her eyes glittering, stiffened.

"Now, Mrs. Burnett, we mustn't have that kind of talk here," Hare said, his voice suddenly harsh.

"That is exactly the kind of talk we are going to have," Val said. She walked to the chair opposite Hare's desk and sat down. "I have been talking to the Chief of Police. He tells me he wants to send you to prison for fourteen years. He seemed quite serious about it."

Hare lowered his bulk back into his chair.

"What he would like to do, Mrs. Burnett and what he can do are two very different things."

Val gazed steadily at him.

"But he can do it. I have only to tell him you and your assistants blackmailed me for you and your assistants to go to prison for fourteen years."

Karsh said hurriedly, "Don't bring me into this . . ."

Hare glared at him.

"Shut up!" To Val he said, "Surely, Mrs. Burnett, I don't have to remind you of the consequences if you confide in Terrell. I admit we would get into trouble, but Terrell could not overlook the fact that your husband is a murderer. I was under the impression that you paid the money to keep that fact quiet."

Val shook her head.

"Oh no, I didn't," she said. "I gave you the money to establish the fact that you were blackmailing me. The police and my bank have the numbers of all the bills. The police know I gave you the money. They would have no difficulty in proving you did blackmail me and your assistants had a part in it."

"Now, wait . . ." Karsh began, sweat breaking out on his face.

"Will you shut up!" Hare barked. "I think you are bluffing, Mrs. Burnett. Am I to understand you don't mind your husband being tried for murder?"

"Oh, yes, I mind," Val said quietly, "but I am not submitting to blackmail. I've thought about it. It is better for my husband to stand trial than to pay blackmail. You hold the only evidence against him : the police will want to know why you didn't give them this evidence : that, coupled with the fact they know I paid you all this money will send you to prison almost as long as the sentence my husband would get."

Hare began to feel uneasy.

"I still think you are bluffing," he said. "Your husband will spend the rest of his days in a criminal asylum."

"It is possible, but we will hire very clever attorneys," Val said. "He could get off sooner than that. I'm not bluffing." She reached across the desk and picked up the telephone receiver. "If you think I am, then I'm calling the Chief of Police."

Karsh shouted, "Stop! Don't do it!"

Val replaced the receiver and looked at Karsh who was glaring at Hare.

"You fat old fool! I warned you! She's got us! Now you shut up for a change. I'm going to handle this!"

Hare, livid, started to say something, but Lucille cut in. "Let him handle it. I said all along I didn't like it."

Hare hesitated, then swung his chair around so his back was to Val. He looked like a man about to have a stroke.

Karsh said, "Mrs. Burnett, I want you to believe neither my wife nor me wanted anything to do with this. Look, we'll give you back the money and the evidence. If we do that, will you forget it? We don't want trouble with the police and you don't want trouble for your husband. That's right, isn't it?"

Hare snarled. "You bird brain! She's bluffing!"

Val looked at Karsh.

"Give me the jacket and the lighter and the money." Her heart was pounding, but she managed to look straight at Karsh although she was a lot more frightened than he. "And I'll forget I've ever been here."

Karsh hurried to the safe. He took out the parcel containing the jacket. To this he added the gold cigarette lighter. Then picking up the brief-case containing the twenty thousand dollars, he handed the three articles to Val.

When she had gone, Hare threw the remains of his chicken sandwich across the office.

"Fools! Couldn't you see she was bluffing? You've let half a million dollars walk out of here!"

"Yeah?" Karsh sneered, pressing the ice-bag against his aching eye, "then why are you wasting good food? If we're going to be all that poor, you'll need every crumb you can find."

Chapter Eleven

MOE HAD remained in the cupboard recess at Fris-Fris's bar until nine o'clock. In the meantime, Fris-Fris had alerted the boys along the water front to report on the activities of the police.

A telephone call at a few minutes to nine assured Fris-Fris the search for Moe had moved on and the immediate district was now clear of police.

He hurried to let Moe out of his hiding place.

" They've gone for the moment," he said as he led Moe into a back room furnished only with a table and four chairs. " So what are you going to do now?"

During the time Moe had been shut up in the darkness he had grieved for Jacko's loss. His grief had been devastating and genuine. He had adored Jacko. Now life without him was as empty to Moe as a hole in a wall. He just could not imagine what he would do with himself without Jacko. It was as if a shutter had slammed shut, cutting off his future existence.

The five thousand dollars he had taken from Hardy's penthouse meant nothing to him. What was money without Jacko?

Fris-Fris watched him anxiously. He had never seen Moe like this before : uncertain, his face haggard, his eyes sightless.

"Moe! Baby! What's the matter?" Fris-Fris asked nervously. "You must think of yourself now. I could get you on a ship. There's one sailing tonight for Jamaica. You have money, haven't you?"

Moe sat on one of his chairs. He put the brief-case containing the five thousand dollars on the table. He stared across the room without apparently hearing what Fris-Fris had said.

"Baby! Come on!" Fris-Fris urged. "They could come back. They knew you and me know each other. We must make a plan."

Moe suddenly snapped out of his mood. He stiffened, and the blank expression in his eyes changed to a murderous burning hate.

"I know what I'm going to do. I'm going to get that slob who killed Jacko!"

Fris-Fris flinched.

"You're crazy! You must get away! Forget Hardy! You must think of yourself!"

"I'm going to fix that slob. I don't care what happens to me so long as I fix him."

Fris-Fris wrung his fat hands.

"We'll fix him, baby. The boys will take care of him. Every cop in town is hunting for you. You get on this ship. I'll arrange everything. You don't have to think of Hardy. The boys will take care of him."

"No one's taking care of him but me!" Moe shouted, hammering the table with his fists. "Anyone who touches that slob is in trouble with me!"

Fris-Fris lifted his hands helplessly.

"All right, baby, but you will never get him. The heat right now is terrible. Every cop . . ."

"Oh, wrap up! Get me a change of clothes . . . something dark and snap it up!"

Fris-Fris had a sudden idea. He was desperately anxious that Moe should escape. His black face lit up.

"I have a girl's outfit here, baby. It would fit you. How's about it? I have a beehive wig too. I'll get you up so your own mother wouldn't know you."

Moe stared, then nodded.

"Now you're talking," he said.

Forty-five minutes later, a slim Jamaican girl, her black beehive hair like a helmet, her blue and yellow dress caught tight at her waist, her bare feet in yellow sandals, walked out of Fris-Fris's bar and along the waterfront.

She was carrying a large yellow and blue handbag: in the bag was a .38 automatic.

Gina and Hardy lay on the big double bed. Hardy was a little drunk. They had just made explosive love, and now Hardy wanted to sleep, but Gina was restless and uneasy.

"Let's talk," she said, stretching her beautiful naked body the way a cat stretches. "Lee! I'm worried sick. They can't do anything to you, can they, for killing that fat beast?"

"No," Hardy said. "It's routine stuff. Harry will take care of it. Don't keep on about it. It was self-defence. Now, relax, can't you? Let's sleep."

"But it's not ten yet," Gina said. "How can I sleep? Let's go somewhere. Let's go to the Coral Club."

Hardy opened his eyes and peered at her.

"If you imagine I'm going out while that black thug is still loose, you're nuts," he said.

Gina's eyes opened wide.

"You mean he might do something to you?"

"What the hell do you think we have a cop outside the front door for?" Hardy asked impatiently. "What the hell do you think we have two cops planted in the lobby downstairs for? They think he'll come up here after me. He and Jacko were husband and wife." He sat up abruptly. "I wish to God I hadn't shot that fat ape. I don't know why I did it."

"But suppose they don't find him?" Gina asked, also sitting up, her eyes alarmed. "You mean we have to stay here until he is caught?"

"Yeah. I'm not going out until they do get him, and they will. Every cop in town is after him."

Gina got off the bed and walked across the room to where her wrap lay on the floor. Hardy studied her nakedness as she moved and as she bent down to pick up the wrap. He had known more women than he could hope to remember. Not one of them excited him as Gina excited him.

"Get me a drink," he said, lying back on the pillow.

Gina went into the kitchen, made two whiskies and added ginger ale and ice. She came back, gave one glass to Hardy, then curled up in a chair near the bed.

"Let's get married, Lee," she said. "I'm sick of drifting around this way. Let's get married. We could even have kids."

Hardy stared at her in amazement, then laughed.

"Coming from you that's a riot. Kids? Who wants kids?"

"I do," Gina said quietly.

After staring at her, Hardy became thoughtful.

"Well, I don't know." He shook his head, but Gina, watching him, saw the suggestion had made an impression.

"We needn't rush it," she said. "The kids I mean, but let's get married."

"Why can't you be happy as you are?" Hardy asked, suddenly on the defensive. "Why should we get married?"

"I've already told one lie for you that could get me into trouble," Gina said. "Now I have to tell another . . . that Jacko was going to kill me so you killed him first. That could also get me into trouble. I don't like trouble, Lee. Why should I stick my neck out for you?" She paused, then went on, "I'd cut my heart out for my husband."

Hardy frowned up at the ceiling. Why not get married? Why not even have a couple of kids?

He suddenly relaxed and grinned.

"Well, okay, Pekie, if that's what you want," he said "I could do worse. It might be an idea at that. Okay, as soon as this mess has been cleared up, we'll do it."

"Don't sound so damned enthusiastic," Gina said and giggled. This was the moment she had been plotting for now for the past three weeks.

"What do you expect me to do?" Hardy asked grinning. "Set fire to the joint?"

Gina gave an excited squeal and springing up, she threw herself on him, knocking his glass flying.

At this moment, a slim Jamaican girl walked down the alley at the back of Hardy's apartment block. She moved quickly and silently, and no one saw her as she gently opened the door that led to the janitor's office. She stepped into the corridor, shut the door and paused to listen. The janitor's office was in darkness. A door at the far end of the corridor stood ajar, and a light came through into the corridor. Moving like a black ghost, she edged towards the stairs as a man in the room cleared his throat noisily. She kept on and reached the first floor. Here she paused as she could see the doorman reading a sporting sheet from behind the desk. She edged to the flight of stairs and again succeeded in moving out of sight without being seen.

On the second floor landing, she pressed the elevator button and when the elevator arrived, she entered and pressed the eighth floor button . . . one floor below Hardy's penthouse. As the elevator took her swiftly upwards, she opened her bag and took from it a flick knife. She touched the button and a long, glittering blade sprang from the handle. The elevator came to rest and the doors swished open. Holding the knife out of sight by her side, she stepped out of the elevator and paused to listen. Hearing nothing, she again started up the stairs. As she reached the head of the stairs, a short, thickset man with cop written all over him, started down the corridor towards her.

"You! Where do you think you're going?" he snapped, off his guard to see a Jamaican girl facing him.

The knife flashed towards him and took him in the throat even as his hand began to move to the gun in his holster. He fell on hands and knees, gurgling. The Jamaican ran swiftly to him and lifting her heavy handbag, slammed it down on his head.

Moe . . . for it was Moe . . . stood staring down at the twitching body of the police officer. Then he bent, recovered his knife, wiped the blade clean on the dead man's coat and returned the knife to the handbag. He then took out the gun and stepping past the dead man, he walked swiftly down the corridor to Hardy's front door. He rang the door bell and stood, waiting, his beehive wig slightly askew, his lips drawn back off his teeth.

"You dope! Look what you have done to my drink!" Hardy was saying as the front door bell rang.

Gina stiffened and looked at Hardy. He sat up, then swung his legs off the bed and struggled into his dressing-gown.

" Who's that?" Gina asked, her eyes growing wide.

" That cop," Hardy said in disgust. " I bet he's trying to cadge a drink." He started towards the bedroom door.

" Lee! Don't go! Let me go!"

" Oh, relax!" Hardy said irritably. " What are you worrying about? We are surrounded by goddamn cops."

He went out into the lobby as the bell rang again.

" Lee!" Gina screamed as Hardy unlocked the front door. *" Lee!"*

The sound of three revolver shots crashed through the penthouse. There was a moment of silence, then the thud of a falling body.

Gina shut her eyes. With an agonised cry, she threw herself face down on the bed.

The two police officers on guard in the lobby were waiting for Moe as he came out of the elevator. It took five bullets to kill him and he died grinning, his beehive wig at the back of his head and his flowered dress rucked up around his black thighs.

A little before eight the following morning, Val surprised the hall-porter at the Spanish Bay hotel by coming onto the terrace, wearing slacks and a halter and carrying a heavy beach bag. He hurried towards her and she gave him a tight, forced smile.

" I thought I'd have an early swim," she said as he took the bag. " It's nice to have the beach to one's self."

The hall-porter, used to the idiosyncrasies of the rich, agreed. He watched her drive away, then shrugging, he returned to his post at the entrance to the hotel.

Val drove along the deserted beach road until she was out of sight of the hotel. She parked the car off the road, then carrying the beach bag, she walked down to the sea, slithering down the high sand dunes until she reached a secluded spot where no one could possible see her.

She dumped the bag and walked around collecting dry wood

that littered that part of the beach. In a while she had made a big pile of wood. From the beach bag she took a large bottle of lighter fuel and a newspaper. She soaked the paper with the fuel, pushed it under the pile of wood. Then she took from the beach bag, Chris's blood-stained jacket. This she also soaked with the lighter fuel. She put the jacket onto the wood pile and striking a match, she tossed the match onto the jacket.

She jumped clear as the whole thing went up in a roaring mass of flames. She stood watching. Within a few minutes the jacket was reduced to grey ashes which the mild wind coming from the sea began to scatter along the beach.

Satisfied that there was nothing left of the jacket, she took off her slacks and ran down, in halter and briefs, to the sea.

She swam for ten minutes, then she came out of the sea and again looked at the funeral pile of the jacket. Again satisfied that there was nothing left of it, she stripped off her bathing things, hurriedly dried herself with a towel, slipped into a light sweater and slacks and fifteen minutes later, she was back in the hotel.

She remained in her suite until eleven o'clock, then wearing a simple white frock and sandals, she drove to the sanatorium.

Dr. Gustave received her in his office.

" I have news for you," he said. " Dr. Zimmerman will be arriving this afternoon. You may not have heard of him, but he is the best brain specialist in the world. I have been in correspondence with him about your husband. He seems to think he can do a lot more for him than I have been able to do. In actual fact, your husband is much better. He is making steady progress, but Zimmerman thinks a small operation on the brain might very easily complete the cure. He is optimistic, but I would rather you weren't. One never knows when dealing with a case like this. Anyway, I am satisfied that Zimmerman can't do any harm : he can only do good."

Val sat motionless, her hands tight in her lap.

" Am I to give a decision?"

Gustave smiled.

" No, I have talked to your husband. He wants the operation

done. Naturally, I am consulting you, but as he wants it, I think you are relieved of any responsibility."

" I'm not afraid of responsibility," Val said. " What happens if the operation isn't successful?"

" According to Zimmerman . . . nothing. I am ready to accept his opinion. It is not a kill or cure thing. Your husband will either make a complete recovery or else he will continue more or less as he is now."

" Then of course, he must have it," Val said. " There would be no danger to him?"

" None at all. Zimmerman has performed the operation successfully a number of times."

" But you are not optimistic?"

" I didn't say that. I don't want *you* to be optimistic."

" And when will it be?"

" Dr. Zimmerman arrives here tomorrow afternoon. The operation will take place the following morning."

Val got to her feet.

" I'll talk to Chris now. Is he in the garden?"

" You'll find him there."

She looked anxiously at him.

" Still guarded?"

Dr. Gustave smiled his professional smile.

" Guarded isn't the right word, Mrs. Burnett. Shall we say he is still being supervised?"

" If this operation is successful, he won't have to be . . . supervised?"

" Of course not."

" But how will you *know* it is successful?"

" There will be various signs." Dr. Gustave's expression became vague. " It may take a few months before we can be absolutely certain of the cure. We can expect to find a marked change once he is up and about again."

They spent a few more minutes talking, then Val went out into the garden.

Chris Burnett was reading under the big tree. The nurse, sitting a few yards from him, was knitting. She nodded and smiled at Val as she saw her coming along the path. Chris looked up, closed his book, after slipping a paper marker into the place where he had been reading. He put the book down and got to his feet. He didn't come towards her, but his smile was a little warmer than the last time they had met and he had taken the trouble, Val noted, to get to his feet.

" Did you hear the news?" he asked, pulling a chair nearer his. " About Zimmerman?"

" Yes." She sat down, longing to touch him. " How do you feel about it, Chris?"

" I'm rather excited." He slumped down into his chair. " I'm getting pretty bored with myself here. If I could only get back to the office again! It's dull just sitting here with her watching me all the time."

" It would be wonderful, wouldn't it?" Val said, trying to sound enthusiastic. " They seem very hopeful. But we mustn't expect a miracle all at once. They did say . . ."

" Oh, I know. They told me." He stared away down the path, frowning. " How's your father?"

" He's fine. Busy as usual. He is telephoning tonight."

" Better not tell him about Zimmerman. You know what your father is. If it doesn't come off, he'll get disagreeable again."

" No, he won't," Val said quickly. " But I needn't tell him if you don't want me to."

" Better not." He looked at her, his eyes probing. " How are we off for money? I suppose we can afford this operation? This chap charges the earth."

" We are quite all right for money."

He hesitated, looking away from her, then he said, " But this blackmailer?"

Val hesitated, then aware of the tension from her husband, she decided to tell him the truth.

" I'm not paying him."

Chris stiffened. His hands suddenly turned into fists. The twitch around his mouth became more pronounced.

" Is that wise? You said you were going to pay him."

"Yes, but I changed my mind. I talked to him again and I decided he was bluffing."

He moved uneasily.

"This could be serious. If I have this operation and I am cured, I don't want to be arrested just when I'm starting a new life."

"Why should you be arrested?"

He again hesitated, then said, "This blackmailer could turn spiteful. I think we should pay him."

"But it doesn't matter if he does turn spiteful. You haven't done anything, Chris, so why should we worry?"

He put his hand to his face to hide the twitching.

"I can't remember what happened on that night. I *could* have done something." He paused, frowning uneasily, then went on, "I get a vague idea sometimes that I did do something."

Val drew in a deep breath. It was some moments before she could control the shake in her voice to ask, "You remember the woman and the elephants?"

"Yes. Why?"

"I've been thinking about her. I wondered if she wore a bracelet with miniature elephants on it and that was why you associated elephants with her."

He looked startled, then he slapped his knee.

"That's clever of you. I remember now. Yes, she did wear a bracelet with elephants on it."

"Did she remind you of a Pekinese dog?"

He stared at her, his eyes narrowing.

"Is she the one who is blackmailing us?"

"No. The other day I saw a girl in the hotel restaurant. She wore this bracelet. She was attractive. She had one of those squashed, attractive puggy faces."

Chris rubbed his face with his hand. He thought for some moments, frowning.

Finally, he said, "Yes: so did this girl. I can see her plainly now."

"You were sorry for her. You told me that," Val said. "Why were you sorry for her?"

"I don't know. Did I say that?" His face suddenly relaxed into blankness. It was as if a shutter had come down between his eyes and his brain, cutting her completely off from him. "I say lots of things I don't mean."

She realised she would only be wasting time trying to get any further information from him and she abruptly began to talk about her morning's swim. He listened politely, but she could see he wasn't interested. After a few minutes of further futile conversation, she got up to go.

"I'll see you tomorrow, Chris. Perhaps I'll be able to talk to Zimmerman."

"You still don't think it would be safer to pay this man?" he asked, peering up at her.

"What man, Chris?"

He made an impatient movement.

"This blackmailer."

"No. I don't."

His long lean fingers moved uneasily over his knees.

"We might be sorry if we don't."

"I still think it would be wrong and stupid to pay him. Why should we?"

The twitch at his mouth jumped like an aching nerve.

"Who is he?"

"A private detective."

Chris flinched.

"That type is always dangerous. We'd better pay him."

"Don't you want to know why he is trying to blackmail us?"

A shifty expression came into Chris's eyes as he shook his head.

"No, I don't want to know. I'm not well. You know that. I don't want to be worried by things." She realised he was now hiding himself behind a smoke screen of unreality. "People say so many disgusting things about other people. I don't want to hear anything like that."

On a sudden impulse, she opened her handbag and took out the gold cigarette lighter. She put it into his hand.

159

" I found this, Chris."

He stared at the lighter, holding it for a brief second. Then he gave a shudder, and with a movement of revulsion, he threw the lighter from him the way a man who finds some loathsome insect on him, gets rid of it.

Then he looked up at her. The expression on his face terrified her. He wasn't Chris any more. He wasn't human any more. He began to move out of his chair as she began to back away from him. His breath came through his clenched teeth in a soft, hissing sound. His hands, his fingers hooked, moved upwards as he got to his feet.

" Chris !"

Her voice was sharp and terrified.

" I've had enough of you," he said, his voice a soft, frightening whisper. " I'm going to kill you the way I killed her !"

Then the nurse was behind him. Her hands gripping his wrists, and with speed and strength, locking them behind him in a Judo grip. She held him powerless while he glared at Val, his mouth working and the awful twitch moving under his skin like the flickering of a snake's tongue.

" Go !" the nurse said urgently. " Tell Dr. Gustave ! Hurry ! I can manage him !"

Val turned and ran blindly back towards the house. At the end of the path she met one of the male attendants who turned as he heard her quick footfalls.

She gasped out what was happening, then as he ran to the nurse's help, she dropped on her knees on the grass and hid her face in her hands.

Chapter Twelve

AT THE time Val was burning her husband's jacket, Terrell was finishing his favourite breakfast of eggs and grilled ham.

A few minutes before he had sat down, Jacobs had driven Mrs. Prescott, Angel and her Teddy Bear from Terrell's bungalow, back to the Park Motel.

Both Terrell and his wife were relieved to see them go. The child had been too much even for Terrell's patience.

As he ate, Terrell looked back on the previous day. Jacko and Moe were now accounted for. He thought with regret of the officer whom Moe had killed. Lee Hardy was dead. Terrell had no regrets about him. With Jacko and Moe out of the way, Henekey's murder could be considered closed. There still remained Sue Parnell's murder to be solved. So far there was not a single clue that might lead him to the killer. Then there was this odd business of Val Burnett paying Homer Hare twenty thousand dollars. Terrell was sure Hare was blackmailing Val Burnett, but there was nothing he could do about that, he told himself, unless she was willing to co-operate.

It was while he was finishing his second cup of coffee that he heard a car pull up outside the bungalow. Glancing through the open window, he saw Joe Beigler and Fred Hess get out of a police car and come striding up his garden path.

" More trouble," he said to Carrie." Now what do they want this time?"

He left the morning-room and opening the front door let Beigler and Hess in.

"What's up now?" he asked as he led the way into the lounge.

"I took Hardy's prints when they dumped him in the morgue," Hess said. "I've been checking all the prints I found in the cabin where the Parnell woman was knocked off. Hardy's prints are on the list. He was definitely in the cabin at some time. While I was at it, I checked Henekey's office. Hardy's prints are also on Henekey's desk."

Terrell moved around the room, puffing at his pipe. Finally, he said, "This could be the answer. That alibi the Lang girl gave Hardy never jelled with me. Could be Hardy did the job. Let's go talk to her."

"I guessed you'd want to do that," Beigler said. "I have a search warrant. If we tear the place apart, we might even turn up the motive."

The three police officers arrived outside Lee Hardy's penthouse front door at a few minutes to nine. Beigler dug his thumb into the bell push and held it there for several seconds, then the three men waited. More seconds dragged past and Beigler again thumbed the bell push.

The front door was suddenly jerked open by Gina, her face like a stone mask and dark smudges under her eyes. She was wearing a flower patterned wrap and her feet were bare. She looked as if she had just got out of bed. By the way she screwed up her eyes as if trying to focus the police officers, Terrell could see she was drunk.

"I want to talk to you," Terrell said and riding her back, he moved into the lobby.

She shrugged indifferently and then walked unsteadily into the lounge. She seemed glad to flop into one of the big comfortable lounging chairs. She rubbed her eyes, yawned and then stared at Terrell without seeing him.

"Make some coffee," Terrell said to Beigler. "She's plastered."

Beigler went out of the room in search of the kitchen. Hess took a chair behind Terrell and fiddled with a notebook while Terrell slowly filled his pipe.

Gina said abruptly, " What is it? If you've just come to stare at me, then get the hell out of here!"

" You told me Hardy spent the evening here with you . . . the evening Sue Parnell was murdered. I'm asking you again : was Hardy here or were you lying?"

" Lee didn't murder her," Gina said.

" I didn't ask you that. I asked if you gave him a false alibi. This is serious. I have reason to believe he was in this woman's cabin at the motel on the night she died."

" What's it matter where he was now? He's dead, isn't he?" Gina, said, lighting a cigarette.

" Did you or did you not lie when you said he was with you on that night?" Terrell demanded, his voice hardening.

" Oh, go to hell! What does it matter? He's dead! He was the only man I ever cared for! He's dead! Get the hell out of here!" She got unsteadily to her feet and started towards the door as Beigler came in, a jug of coffee in one hand, a cup in the other. " And you . . . clear out too!" Gina screamed at him. She gave him a violent push so that the jug of coffee flew out of his hand, smashing against the wall. The coffee streamed down the wall as Gina, dodging around Beigler, ran into her bedroom and slammed the door.

Beigler smothered an expletive and then put the cup on the occasional table. He looked at Terrell.

" Leave her be for the moment," Terrell said. " Let's look around and see if we can find a motive for the killing."

Methodically, the three men began to search the penthouse, avoiding Gina's room. It was Hess, a couple of hours later, searching Hardy's bedroom who found what they were looking for. In a large envelope, tucked behind a reproduction of a Picasso design, above Hardy's bed, was a thin leather-bound diary, a folded letter addressed to Gina, and two cancelled cheques of five thousand dollars each made out to " Bearer ".

Terrell sat on the bed and read the letter.

Dear Pekie,

If anything should happen to me, turn the contents of this envelope over to the police. Sue found out about the reefer racket I'm snarled up in, and she's been squeezing me ever since I threw her out. She got hold of the duplicates of the records and she has enough to put me away for ten years. She is set to squeeze me dry, but if I walk under a car or something, I want her to pay for the merry hell she's cooked up for me. Give Terrell the diary and the cheques. If he can't fix her, no one can.

Lee

Terrell spent sometime going through the diary, then he looked over at Beigler who was smoking and sipping coffee he had made while Terrell was occupied.

"Here's the motive. He got tired of paying, so he knocked her off. He ripped her to make it look like a sex killing," Terrell said. "Now, I'll talk to her."

"You're welcome," Beigler said. "Want me along?"

"What do you think?" Terrell got to his feet, and followed by Beigler, he walked from the lounge and into Gina's bedroom.

They found Gina, now dressed, sitting on the edge of the bed, a glass half full of whisky in her hand.

"The Parnell woman was blackmailing Hardy," Terrell said. "We have proof here." He waved the diary and the letter. "Now come on: you lied when you said he was here on the night she died, didn't you?"

Gina frowned at the whisky in the glass, then suddenly, she shrugged.

"So what does it matter? So I lied," she said, "but he didn't kill her. You're not pinning murder on him even if he is dead."

Terrell sat down. His slight signal alerted Beigler who moved over to the window, sat down and took out his notebook.

"If you're so sure about that, who did kill her?" Terrell asked.

"Oh, a guy," Gina said. "He was a nut. I didn't know he had screws loose at first, but it has gradually dawned on me."

"Just what are you talking about?" Terrell asked, leaning forward. "Who is this man? What do you know about him?"

"A guy I ran into," Gina said. She blew out her cheeks and moved a strand of hair off her face. Terrell could see she was very drunk now.

"Suppose we begin at the beginning? Where do you come in on this?"

"I found the letter and the diary the way you found it," Gina said, staring glassily at her drink. "I guessed Lee was having trouble with that bitch, but it wasn't until I found the letter and the dairy that I realised she was set to squeeze him dry. I wanted to marry him. I loved him, so I decided to fix her. If he was to spend his money on anyone it was to be me . . . certainly not her. One evening when he thought I was out, he called her. I listened in on the extension. They made a date at the Park Motel. He was paying her another five thousand. So I decided to go out there and persuade her to part with the records she had stolen from him." She got unsteadily to her feet, weaved across the room, opened a drawer in a closet and took from it a broad bladed hunting knife. She came back and offered it, hilt first, to Terrell.

"I took this along with me. My idea was to knock her out, tie her up and threaten to carve her face to bits. I would have done it too, but I guessed she would part with what she had stolen before I had to start on her."

Terrell examined the knife. There were dark stains near the hilt. He put it carefully on the bedside table before saying, "Then what happened?"

"After Lee left the motel, I picked up a U-Drive car. I didn't intend to kill her, but if she wouldn't play, I was ready to go the whole way and I wanted to be sure no one could trace me so I didn't use my own car." She paused, wiped her flushed face with the back of her hand and looked over at Beigler. "Am I going too fast for you?"

"You're doing great," Beigler said sarcastically.

"Why take a U-Drive car? You'd have to show your licence," Terrell said.

Gina sneered at him.

"You think I'm that dopey? I stole a handbag off some girl and used her licence. I even bought a blonde wig." She paused to sip the whisky, then went on, "I gave Lee half-an-hour's start, then I drove after him. I was within ten miles of the Park Motel, driving slow because I didn't want to run into Lee and besides, I was tight, when a man walked right in front of the car. I stopped fast, but he was close enough for the fender to be touching him, when I did stop." She peered at Terrell. "You don't have to believe any of this. I can't prove it."

"Keep going," Terrell said.

"Well, this guy asked for a lift. I said I was going to Ojus and he said that would be fine with him. So he got in. I had had a good look at him in the headlights and he wasn't the kind who would worry me. Anyway, few men worry me. I know how to handle men. But this guy was something special. He was a looker: a real doll." She paused to sip her whisky, then went on, "There was something about him that made me want to confide in him. I was drunker than a skunk and weepy. I had to be drunk if I was going to do what I planned to do. Okay, I guessed I talked too much. I told him about Lee. I told him about the Parnell bitch. I told him I had to get these papers from her or kill her. By the time I started shooting my mouth off, we had arrived at the Park Motel. Then he started talking as we sat in the car in the motel's parking lot. He said he would take care of everything. He said he liked me: he was sorry for me: he knew what it was to be in love. He had lots of authority, looks and confidence. I was so goddamn drunk I was glad to listen to him. He said women like Sue Parnell weren't fit to live. He said he would take care of her. On the back seat of the car I had left the knife and a tyre lever. He took them. As he got out of the car, I suddenly got scared. I said I didn't want him to do anything. I could handle it. He smiled at me. 'You couldn't fly a kite,' he said. By this time the drink was really hitting me. I knew if I got out of the car, I couldn't even stand. I let him go and sat in the car, waiting. After a while he came back and got in the car. He said, ' I've fixed it.' By this time, I was ready to pass out. I had a pint in the car and I kept hitting it. I felt him push me into the passenger seat, and then I felt the car move. I guess I passed out. The next thing I remember was waking up on the grass verge of the highway. He and the car had disappeared." She again blew out her cheeks and passed her hand across her face. "Gee! I'm tight! That's all. Lee never killed her. It was this guy."

"How do you know he killed her?" Terrell asked. "Hardy could have killed her and this guy you talk about could have walked in and found her."

"Think so? I say different. When he went into the cabin he was wearing a sports jacket. When he came out, he was carrying the jacket, inside out . . . why? He gave me the knife. It was wrapped up in her pants. He said, ' You're lucky. I've fixed it. You have no more worries the way I have.' I found the knife and her pants in my handbag the following morning when I got sober. There was blood in my bag, on the knife and the pants. I put the bag and pants into the basement furnace . . . he killed her all right."

"Let's look at it another way," Terrell said. " Suppose this convenient nut never existed? Suppose you went into the cabin and failing to make Sue Parnell part, you killed her. That would be a lot more simple, wouldn't it?"

Gina finished her drink. She sneered at Terrell as she put down her glass.

"That's a cop all over. You hear so many lies, you don't believe the truth when you hear it."

"I like it better this way. I think you're trying to talk yourself out of a murder rap."

"That's right. Take it the easy way," Gina said. " It would suit you to pin this on me, wouldn't it? You wouldn't have to look further. You wouldn't have to hunt for this boy-friend, would you?"

"For the record," Terrell said, "let's have something more

about his boy-friend. If you saw him again, would you recognise him?"

" I'd know him anywhere. He was the kind you couldn't help but know again . . . a real doll!"

" Let's have something to work on: what was he like: give me a description of him."

" He was tall, handsome and dark. He had everything. He was sympathetic. He was the kind of man you would tell your frankest secrets to."

" You said he was a nut. Why do you say that?"

" Of course he was a nut. He wouldn't have gone in there and ripped her unless he was a nut. I provided him with an excuse to kill a woman. I guess I was lucky he didn't kill me."

Terrell looked at Beigler who lifted his shoulders. Gina's story sounded as corny to him as it did to Terrell.

" I still think Hardy could have done it and you're drunk enough to dream up this story," Terrell said. " But you'll come to headquarters and we'll work all this over. Come on . . . let's go."

Gina grimaced.

" My road stopped when Lee died," she said. " I've had all I want from life and it hasn't been all that hot. Lee didn't kill her. Can't you get that fact into your thick skull? It was this nut who did it."

" We'll go over it again at headquarters. Let's go," Terrell said getting to his feet.

Gina shrugged and stood up.

" Excuse me while I spend a dime," she said. " My back teeth are floating." She walked unsteadily across the bedroom and into the bathroom. As she shut the door, Terrell said, " What do you make of this story, Joe?"

" She's lying," Beigler said. " It's my bet . . ."

The violent bang of a gun, coming from the bathroom made both men start to their feet. As one, they rushed to the bathroom door. Beigler drove his massive shoulder against the panel and burst in.

Gina lay face down on the floor, a smoking gun in her hand.

Her brains made a white and red stain on the bathroom tiles.

As Terrell came in from a quick lunch, he met Beigler, looking hot and irritable, getting out of his car. The two men walked fast up the steps into police headquarters.

"How's it coming?" Terrell asked as he led the way to his office.

"Got something," Beigler said. He entered the office and lowered his heavy frame onto one of the upright chairs. Terrell went behind his desk and sat down. He poured coffee from the flask.

"Go ahead."

"The day before the murder, a woman, Ann Lucas, reported her handbag stolen. That afternoon, a woman calling herself Ann Lucas hired a car from the U-Drive Depot for five days. The guy who handled the deal wouldn't know her again without the sun goggles and the scarf she was wearing. It's my bet this woman was Gina Lang."

Terrell rubbed the end of his nose with the butt of his pen.

"So she wasn't lying."

"That's it, but here's something you're going to love," Beigler said. "Sam Karsh turned up at the U-Drive joint two days after the murder. He told them he had found one of their cars . . . the car rented by Ann Lucas or Gina Lang . . . dumped in a clearing on a dirt road off the North Miami Beach highway. He told Morphy . . . he's the manager of the joint . . . he had found the car and thought it had been dumped. He asked questions, got a description of this Ann Lucas or Gina Lang and then faded away. I've contacted Ann Lucas. She tells me that on the night Karsh contacted Morphy, she got a mysterious telephone call from a guy who questioned her about the loss of her driving licence. After she had admitted losing her licence and as soon as she began questioning him, he hung up. That could have been Karsh."

Terrell said, "What are we waiting for? Let's get Karsh here."

169

Beigler grinned.

"Jacobs is already picking him up. He loves Karsh."

"Okay, Joe, nice work. I want to think about all this. When Karsh arrives let him sweat it out. I may not be ready for him for an hour."

When Beigler had gone, Terrell sat for some time thinking, then he abruptly reached forward and flicked down a switch on the inter-com.

"I want the file covering Chris Burnett's disappearance," he said.

When an officer brought in the file, Terrell studied it. Then he took a large scale map of the district from his desk drawer and studied that.

The inter-com came to life.

"We have Karsh here, Chief," a voice said.

"Let him stew. I'm not ready for him yet."

Terrell sat for another half-hour going over the file, making notes, studying the map, then he called for Beigler.

Beigler came in, sat down and lit a cigarette. He looked expectantly at Terrell.

"This could be a sweet one," Terrell said, pushing back his chair and crossing his legs. "I'm getting persuaded that Chris Burnett killed Sue Parnell."

Beigler sucked his cigarette, his eyes widening.

"You tell it," he said.

"We know Burnett is a nut. Gina Lang claims to have picked up a nut who was tall, dark and handsome. That description fits Burnett. The time he was missing and the time she picked him up also jells. He was picked up by our men about a mile from where Morphy claims the U-Drive car was dumped. We know Karsh found the car. We know Burnett wore a jacket when he left the hotel and it was missing when he was found. It's my bet Karsh found the jacket in the car and there was blood on it. You don't rip a woman the way Parnell was ripped without getting messy. It looks to me that Karsh took the jacket to Hare who promptly put the bite on Mrs. Burnett. This would explain why she parted with twenty thousand dollars. Why else should she give him that amount of money unless he had her where he wanted her?"

Beigler whistled.

"Can we prove any of this, Chief?"

"Not yet, but we'll have Karsh in and we'll sweat him until he does talk."

"But suppose he doesn't?"

The telephone bell interrupted what Terrell was about to say. He lifted the receiver.

"Thresby here," the manager of the Florida Banking Corporation said. "I thought you would be interested. This morning, Mrs. Burnett paid the twenty thousand dollars back into her account . . . the money we thought was blackmail money."

Terrell scowled and ran his fingers through his greying hair.

"The same numbers?"

"Yes. She paid in the exact bills we issued to her."

"Thanks. I don't know what it means, but it looks as if we've got off to a false start."

"That's what I think. Suppose we forget it? A man like Travers . . . you know what I mean."

"Yeah. Okay, Henry, be seeing you and thanks for calling." Terrell hung up.

"So what now?" Beigler asked.

"Mrs. Burnett paid the money she gave to Hare back into her account . . . so that lets Hare out. Now, why in hell, did she do that? How did she manage to get the money away from Hare?"

"Do we still talk to Karsh?"

Terrell hesitated.

"We haven't a thing to go on. We can't bring a charge against Hare for blackmail now. If we start something we can't finish with Burnett, we'll have Travers on our necks. Don't let's rush this." He picked up his pen and began to make holes in his blotter with it. "Has the U-Drive car been checked for prints?"

171

" Sure . . . it's been wiped clean. No prints."

" If we could find Burnett's prints in the motel cabin we would be getting somewhere. Did you check the knife for prints?"

" Only the Lang woman's and yours."

" Send Jacobs to Gustave's sanatorium right away. Tell him to see Gustave and get Gustave to give him something Burnett has handled. Then get Hess to check through his list of prints in the cabin and see if Burnett was there."

Beigler left the office. Terrell kept making holes in his blotter until Beigler returned.

" He's on his way. How's about Karsh?"

" Yeah. Let's talk to the creep. Maybe he'll open up."

" Maybe: the same way as he'll join the Salvation Army," Beigler said.

Karsh was brought in. He was pale, worried and jumpy.

Terrell asked him about the U-Drive car.

" So what's it to you?" Karsh demanded indignantly. " I'm getting sick of the way you cops keep shoving me around. I happened to be driving in the district and I found the car. I told this jerk it looked as if it were dumped. Can't I do another guy a good turn without you stamping all over me?"

" How did you find it?"

" I tell you . . . I was driving around. The frigging car was dumped. I was curious . . . it's my nature to be curious . . . so I checked the tag, found it belonged to the U-Drive outfit and as I was passing, I dropped in and told them. I was doing them a good turn."

" Imagine you doing anyone a good turn," Beigler sneered. " If you think we believe a yarn like that, you need your head examined."

" Okay, so I need my head examined."

" What did you find in the car, Karsh?" Terrell demanded, leaning across the desk and glaring at Karsh.

" What do you mean? I didn't find a goddamn thing!"

" I think you did. You found a sports jacket with blood on it!"

172

Karsh was too wily a bird to be caught with that one. Although sweat began to appear on his narrow forehead, he went through the act of looking amazed.

"Blood? Jacket? Look, Chief, honest to God I don't know what you're talking about!"

"There was a blood-stained jacket in the back of that car and you found it!"

"I found nothing! I don't know what you're talking about! If I had found anything, I'd have turned it over to you. I saw this car, I thought it was dumped. I tipped off the U-Drive people." Karsh shifted in his chair. "I swear to God . . ."

"You found out the name of the woman who hired the car and you telephoned her, didn't you?"

Karsh rolled his eyes.

"Wait a minute . . . just out of curiosity, I did ask Morphy who had rented the car, but I didn't telephone her. Where did you get that from?"

"You telephoned this woman and you asked if she had lost her driving licence, didn't you?"

"Not me, Chief. You're confusing me with someone else. Not me."

For the next hour, Terrell and Beigler battered away at Karsh, but they didn't break him. Finally, in disgust, Terrell had to admit defeat. He had no proof. He was sure Karsh was lying, but he knew he was wasting his time trying to get him to admit anything.

"Get him out of my sight!" he said finally and walked over to the window, turning his back on Karsh as Beigler hustled him out.

There was another irritating wait, then Hess came in.

"Nothing, Chief," he said. "Jacobs gave me Burnett's prints, but they don't show on my list."

Terrell grunted and waved him away. He looked over at Beigler who was drinking coffee.

"Well, that's it. It's my bet Burnett did the job, but we can't nail it onto him . . . anyway, not yet. Maybe not ever."

Beigler picked up the Sue Parnell file.

" We keep this open then?"

" That's it," Terrell said as he began to fill his pipe. " You never know. We may have some luck. I don't know how long he'll stay in the sanatorium. As long as he's there, he's safe, but if he comes out, he could do it again. If he does, then we'll have him. These killers usually try it again. Yes . . . keep the file open."

Dr. Adolf Zimmerman was short and excessively fat. His eyes, like green gooseberries, dwelt behind horn rimmed, thick lensed glasses. He had the quiet soothing manner of a priest in a confessional box.

He came into the lounge where Val had been waiting for the past two hours. She had heard a murmur of voices outside the door before he came in. She had heard Dr. Gustave say, " If you would rather talk to her alone . . . then go ahead," and she had flinched, feeling sure the operation had failed. But when Zimmerman came in to find her tense and white-faced, he smiled assuringly.

" I am satisfied the operation is a success," he said. " Now don't look so worried. I am sorry to have been so long, but I have to work very carefully." He sat down near her. " I won't bother you with technical details, but your husband is going to be quite normal in a few weeks. There was pressure on the brain. This has been removed. It should have been done before. It would have saved you a lot of anxiety. I wish I had been consulted sooner. However, it is done now."

Val drew in a deep breath.

" You really mean he will be normal again?"

" Yes. In two weeks, he can leave here. I think it would be a good idea for you two to go right away somewhere . . . a sea trip. Why not the South of France? Relax, laze, get to know each other again. Then when you return, all this will be in the past . . . forgotten. You will be able to start a new life together . . . it will be exciting."

" There is no chance that he will ever become violent?"

Zimmerman smiled. He looked very sure of himself. Again

174

Val was reminded of a well fed priest giving comfort to a penitent.

"I can understand that question. You are frightened. Of course . . . that was an unpleasant moment for you. It was caused by pressure . . . the pressure is no longer there. I assure you . . . you have nothing to worry about."

Val thought of the blood-stained jacket that was now white ashes disintegrated by the wind. *Nothing to worry about.* She knew now, in spite of her faith in Chris, that he had killed this woman. Even this news that Chris would be normal again couldn't take the cold fear away that some day the police might find out he had done this awful thing.

Zimmerman got to his feet.

"I have a plane to catch. I arrive . . . I leave . . . I never seem to have any time for myself. Don't worry about anything. Have patience. In two weeks, you and your husband can be completely carefree. I envy you, Mrs. Burnett. It is always an adventure to begin life again."

When he had gone, and as she was about to leave the room, Dr. Gustave came in.

"Well, Mrs. Burnett," he said, smiling at her, "you must be relieved. In a few days you may see your husband. Dr. Zimmerman is very confident. I think you can look forward now to a future of happiness."

But there was something in his manner that made Val look sharply at him.

"Dr. Zimmerman tells me Chris will be quite normal again," she said. "He said there was pressure . . ."

"Dr. Zimmerman is always optimistic," Gustave said quietly. "He has to be. I am less optimistic because I see so many after effects of difficult brain operations. We are fortunate if we are successful in one case out of three. So I don't want you to be too hopeful until Chris is ready to leave here. The next two weeks will tell us what to expect. Even then, we can never be entirely sure. A lot depends on the patient."

"So you don't think he's really cured?" Val said, feeling a chill crawl up her spine.

" I didn't say that. We just don't know. We must wait and see. I don't want you to have any false impressions. I think in about two weeks, I'll be able to tell you better."

As Val walked down the steps of the sanatorium towards her car, she experienced a cold, hollow feeling of fear at the thought of meeting her husband again.

Chapter Thirteen

September 3rd.

*I haven't written up this diary now for more than a month.
I just haven't had any reason to keep a day-to-day account
of what has been happening to me since Chris left the sanatorium.*

*That fat old brain specialist said it was always an adventure
to begin life again. But is it? What kind of an adventure?
He promised Chris would become normal. I suppose he is,
but he isn't the man I married. I can't help it . . . and I do
try . . . but I keep thinking of that woman. Her memory . . .
the awful way she died, makes it impossible for me to continue to love him. Every time I look at his slim, fine hands,
I think of the knife hacking at that woman.*

*I was glad he didn't want to go to the South of France. I
am sure now I couldn't have faced such a trip with him alone.
When he suggested we should come back to the Spanish Bay
hotel and spend two more weeks here while he convalesced.
I was relieved. We have been here now for ten days. We do a
lot of bathing. We sit in the sun. We read. Chris is back on
Dickens again. I am sure he knows that I know he killed this
woman. We can't relax together. We're polite. We smile at
each other. We are both very anxious not to disagree with anything either of us say. I now know it can never be the same as
it was before this ghastly accident. He tells me how anxious
he is to return to New York. Dr. Gustave doesn't want him to
go back for another week. He looks curiously at Chris when*

177

*he comes here to talk to him. I have this feeling he isn't sure
about the operation, but he won't commit himself . . . what
doctors ever do? I walked with him to his car yesterday. Chris
watched us from the terrace. Dr. G said I mustn't expect too
much . . . what does that mean?*

*Last night . . . I suppose this really is why I have begun to
write up this diary again . . . after Chris and I had sat on
the terrace, watching the moon light up the sea . . . he came
to my room. He wanted to make love to me. This was the
first time he had these feelings for me for more than two
years. During those two years I had lain in my lonely bed, aching for him, aching for him to take me, to feel him move into
my body, to feel his face against mine. But seeing him come
into the room, lit only by the moon. I felt terrified. I thought
of his hands and the knife and the woman. He sat on the side
of the bed and he put his hands in mine. But the touch of his
hands turned me cold and sick. I suppose the expression on my
face warned him to go no further. He smiled at me . . . I
thought of Mona Lisa . . . it was that kind of smile, and he
said, ' We'll get adjusted. You've been patient with me. I can
be patient too.' But I felt that he was disappointed and even
suddenly bored with me. When he had gone back to his room,
I cried. I now know I can never bear him to touch me. Is this
what that fat old man calls an adventure to begin life
again?*

September 6th.

*We were sitting together on the terrace when this girl came
down the steps of the hotel. She was quite lovely: young,
golden with the sun, wearing a bikini and her hair was the
colour of honey. She walked with an assurance that I have
never been able to acquire. She was practically naked. The
fold of her buttocks and the thrust of her breasts were something that stabbed me with envy. She went down to her car.
She slid under the wheel, knowing everyone, including Chris
and myself were watching her.*

178

*Chris said, " Did you see that girl? I wonder who she is?
Did you notice the way she moved?"*

I said stupidly, " What girl ? No, I didn't notice."

*It was a lie, and he knew it was a lie. He turned a page of
his book. Secretly watching him, I could see he wasn't reading.
In spite of the sun, I felt suddenly cold.*

It was their last day at the Spanish Bay hotel. Val was busy
packing. Tomorrow morning, they would be flying back to
New York. Chris was on the terrace, reading *Little Dorrit*. As
Val was closing the last suitcase, the telephone bell buzzed.

It was her father.

" Val? All well?"

" Yes, daddy. We leave on the ten o'clock plane."

" Fine. I'll be at the airport to meet you. How's Chris?"

" He's wonderful. He can't wait to get back to the office."

" Is that right? But *how* is he, Val? Look, I'm not sold on that
fat quack. Is Chris *really* all right?"

" But, daddy. what are you saying? Of course he's all right!
He's now ready to start work again."

" Well . . . all right . . . if you say so . . . I talked to Zimmerman. I didn't like him. He's too sure of himself. I don't like
people who are *that* sure of themselves."

Val closed her eyes. She knew from past experience that her
father was always right.

" Darling, Chris is fine. *Do* stop worrying. We'll be back tomorrow. You'll see . . . Chris is really fine."

" And you, Val? How about you?"

She suddenly felt a wave of emotion rush through her. She
couldn't speak. She felt tears running down her face.

" Val! I said how about you?" her father said impatiently.

" I'm—I'm fine too," she said. " Thanks for calling, daddy. I—I
look forward to seeing you," and she replaced the receiver.

She sat crying for several minutes, then she touched her eyes
with her handkerchief and got to her feet. She remembered what
Chris had once said :

Your father is a remarkable man. He hasn't got the soft centre that I have . . . you know what I mean: a soft centre? It is something that can happen to anyone who is just ordinary. You think you are all right, that you are making a big success of life, that you have all the confidence, ambition and determination to beat the best, then suddenly the hard core that is in you to get anywhere in this life, turns soft. That's what has happened to me.

He had advised her to divorce him. She now knew she would have to get the divorce. This dead and mutilated woman lay between them for ever. Yes, she would have to get a divorce. She thought of the years ahead of her. She would, of course, go back to her father's house. At least, that would give him pleasure. And Chris? What would become of him?

She got to her feet and went to the window and looked down on the terrace. The blonde girl in her red bikini was sitting by Chris. The sun lit up her hair. She was laughing and she was very animated. Chris was laughing too. He looked happier than Val had seen him since the accident.

Suddenly he got to his feet and extended his hand. The girl grasped it and stood up. Together they walked along the terrace and down the steps towards the beach.

Val had a feeling that at least Chris's adventure to begin a new life could be beginning.

She went back to the suitcases and began to re-pack, putting her things in one suitcase and his in another.

》》》 If you've enjoyed this book and would like to discover more great vintage crime and thriller titles, as well as the most exciting crime and thriller authors writing today, visit: 》》》

The Murder Room
Where Criminal Minds Meet

themurderroom.com